Advance Praise for *Duty Free*

"This is a wildly entertaining book but, beware, it also bites."

—Neel Mukherjee

"Refreshing, humorous, irreverent, and satirical, Moni Mohsin's *Duty Free* is more than a boy-meets-girl story. It is an insightful social commentary."

—Bharti Kirchner, author of *Darjeeling* and *Pastries*

"A deliciously funny book starring a clueless socialite heroine with inner savvy and a heart of gold. While this sharp, hilarious spoof of upper-class life is set against a backdrop of political unrest in Lahore, Pakistan, Moni Mohsin's lively, witty satire will appeal to a wide readership."

—Anjali Banerjee, author of *Haunting Jasmine*

DUTY FREE

Duty Free

A NOVEL

MONI MOHSIN

Broadway Paperbacks

NEW YORK

Published in slightly different form in paperback in India by
Random House Publishers India Pvt. Ltd., Noida, and in Great Britain
by Chatto & Windus, an imprint of the Random House Group Limited,
London, as *Tender Hooks*.

Library of Congress Cataloging-in-Publication Data

Mohsin, Moni.
   Duty free : a novel / Moni Mohsin. — 1st ed.
      p. cm.
   1. Upper class—Pakistan—Fiction.   2. Arranged marriage—
Fiction.   3. Lahore (Pakistan)—Fiction.   I. Title.

   PR6113.O37D88 2011
   823'.92—dc23

                                                    2011026253

ISBN 978-0-307-88924-9

Printed in the United States of America

Cover design by Jessie Sayward Bright
Cover photography by Getty Images

1   3   5   7   9   10   8   6   4   2

First Broadway Paperbacks Edition

For Shazad, Laila, and Faiz

DUTY FREE

27 *September*

Yesterday was my cousin Jonkers' thirty-seventh birthday. You know Jonkers, *na*? He's my Aunty Pussy's one and only child. Her sun and air. And since I'm doing my whole family tree, now let me tell about Aunty Pussy also. Aunty Pussy is Mummy's cousin. Their mummies were real sisters. If I was English I'd say Jonkers was my first cousin once removed. As if cousins were bikini lines, once removed, twice removed, hundred times removed but still there. And Uncle Kaukab is Jonkers' father. And also Aunty Pussy's husband. Might as well be clear, no? Never know, otherwise, how much people understand and how much people don't understand.

Haan, so where was I? Yes, Jonkers. To celebrate his birthday, Aunty Pussy took us all—Mummy, me, her, and Jonkers also—to Cuckoo's Restaurant for dinner in the old bit of the city next to the Badshahi Mosque. I like Cuckoo's because everyone says it's fab. Foreigners *tau* just love coming here. Or they did before the suicide bombs started in Lahore also. It's a bit bore that Cuckoo's is in the old city, with its bad toilet smells and all its crumbly, crumbly, old, old houses but at least all those prostitutes who used to live nearby in the Diamond Market have gone off to Defence Housing

1

Society to live in neat little *kothis* their politician and feudal boyfriends have bought them. So no chance, thanks God, of bumping into bad-charactered-types. Unless it's suicide bombers, of course. But them *tau* you can bump into anywhere, thanks to the army which has given *jihadis* safe heavens all over Pakistan.

And also it's a bit bore that you have to climb fifty-five thousand steps to get on top of Cuckoo but view from there is fab. You can look right inside the coatyard of the mosque. But we couldn't because there was so much of smog. Lahore has just three problems: traffic, terrorists, and smog. Otherwise *tau* it's just fab.

Anyways, Aunty Pussy had also invited Janoo (he's my husband, *na*) but Janoo was in his bore village, Sharkpur. Okay, okay, I suppose it's *our* village because I'm his wife and what is his is ours, but thanks God I'm not from there and I haven't been there for three years. Janoo spends half his time there, sewing his crops and looking after his mango and orange and grapefruit orchids, sorry, sorry I meant orchards. But because I don't sew the crops, and I only spend the money we get from the crops, it's best for me to live in Lahore where the shops are. Aunty Pussy also invited my darling, shweetoo baby Kulchoo but he said he was doing homework. His GCSEs are on top of his head but I think so he was reading Facebook. Such a little bookworm my baby is.

So us four went and dinner was nice and all but when Jonkers went down the fifty-five thousand steps to pay the bill, Aunty Pussy suddenly resolved into tears. She started weeping into her chicken *tikka*—actually just chicken bones, because she'd eaten up every last bit of the meat. She's very careful that way, Aunty Pussy. She said how her heart wept tears of blood each time she saw poor Jonkers on his own, without wife, without kids and what would happen to him when she died. I wanted to say that after you die he will play *holi* with all that money you have lying in your bank account that you were too much of a meanie to let him enjoy in your lifetime. But I didn't say because it doesn't look nice.

And then she suddenly reached across the table, grabbed my hand in her thin, spidery one and said, "Promise me, promise that you will help me get my Jonky married by the end of the year."

"*Haw*, Aunty—" I began.

But she gripped my hand tighter and shrieked, "Promise!"

"Pussy!" Mummy hissed. "People are looking."

But Aunty Pussy ignored her. "Promise me!" she said in a horse whisper, her nails digging like little blades into my palms and her eyes boaring into mine.

"Okay, okay, Aunty, I promise." I said it to get my hand back really, but the minute she'd let go and sat back in her seat, Aunty Pussy said calmly, "Now remember you've sworn on your child's life."

"*Haw*! I never," I gasped.

"No need to be so dramatical, Pussy," Mummy said.

"When you said promise that's what I said in my heart. So that's what you've promised," said Aunty Pussy, smiling a catty smile.

Before I could reply Jonkers came back up huffing and puffing like the Khyber Mail. And then, naturally, nobody could say anything.

When she dropped me home, Aunty Pussy rolled down her window and shouted, "Remember your promise."

28 September

Look at Aunty Pussy. What a double-crosser! Imagine, doing that to your very own niece. Making such horrid, horrid promises like that in her heart and then pretending that I'd agreed. I called up Mummy first thing this morning and I *tau* told her straight that not even my shoe is going to lift its toe for Aunty Pussy after what she did to me last night. And Mummy said "Think it through" and I said I've thought it through already, thank you very much. *Aik tau* Mummy is also such a side-taker. Honestly. Sometimes I wonder if she knows whose Mummy she is. Mine or Jonkers'?

Today is 28 September. That means Jonkers has two and half months to get married in. Because I think so Muharram begins in middle of December and nobody gets married in Pakistan then, not even Christians, it being Islamic month of mourning and all. So Auntie Pussy has two months to find a bride for Jonkers. She'd better start looking, no?

And me? I'm off to Mulloo's coffee party. All the girls are coming. Bubble, Sunny, Baby, Faiza, Nina. I'm wearing my new cream Prada shoes I got from Dubai, so everyone can see and my new cream outfit I've had made to match. I put on green contacts (blue is so past it) and my new Tom Ford red

5

lipstick and now I'm looking just like Angelina Jolly. But like her healthier, just slightly older sister. I know I shouldn't do my own praises but facts are facts, no? Pity Janoo is not Brad Pitts. But you can't have everything in life, as Mother Rosario used to say at my convent school.

29 *September*

Hai, you won't believe what happened yesterday. I don't think
so I can believe even now. I was sitting in Mulloo's drawing
room sipping coffee and gently swinging my Prada-*wallah* foot
under Sunny's nose so she shouldn't miss that it's from the
new collection and not from old, chatting to her about
importance of baggrounds, when suddenly my mobile started
playing "*Tum Paas Aaye.*" That's my ringing tone *na*, from *Kuch
Kuch Hota Hai*, my most best Bollywood film. The call was
from Kulchoo's school. His stuppid housemaster calling to say
that my poor baby had been hit on the head with a cricket
ball and that his head had got cracked and he had fainted but
now he'd come around and not to worry he seemed okay but
would I like to come and pick him up? Head cracked, fainted,
not to worry. *Not to worry?* For a few moments, I *tau* passed
away myself. When I came too, the girls were all gathered
round me saying "*Hai*, what happened?" I told them what
happened and Sunny said, "My son had *three* fatal accidents
while playing polo and *mashallah* he's still fine, touch wood."

Just look at her, she does so much of competition. Not
cricket but polo. And not one fatal accident but three.

Got Muhammad Hussain—my driver, who else?—to drive

7

me to Kulchoo's school at top speed. From the car only I called Psycho, Janoo's younger sister. Okay, okay her name is Saiqa but I've always called her Psycho because it suits her personality nicer than Saiqa. Her husband's brother is a doctor, *na*, at Omar Hospital and I screamed down the phone at Psycho and said to her, I said, "Psycho if you want to inherit those twelve gold bangles of your mother's that you have your eye on, get your brother-in-law to be standing in the porch when I arrive at the hospital." *Aik tau* she's also so stuppid. Asked lot of stuppid, stuppid-type questions like "What happened, Bhaabi?" and "Which gold bangles?" Such a time-waster.

Poor darling Kulchoo was sitting in his school looking dazed like he'd just jumped off a merry-go-around. He had a towel with ice in it, pressed to his forehead. I threw the filthy towel on the ground (God knows which, which boys from what, what homes had used it before him), threw the housemaster filthy looks, and took Kulchoo straight forward to Omar Hospital where I marched up to the counter and shouted that Psycho's brother-in-law was my sister-in-law's brother-in-law and that I demand to see him there and then.

Thanks God, Kulchoo didn't argue with me and get all embarrassed like he always does when I jump cues and demand to see the top man. I think so my poor shweetoo was too out off it. Finally Psycho's brother-in-law came and did a city-scan and an X-ray and an MRI of my baby's head and said he had a mild-type crack. "Con-cushion," he called it. I called Janoo when we got home and said Kulchoo had had an accident and had got a con-cushion in his head and that he should come back. "Why? How? When?" Janoo barked down the phone. *Uff Allah! Aik tau* he's also so inquisitive. Anyways, I think so, he's coming back tonight, thanks God.

Then I called Mummy and told her what had happened. She was silent for a long time and then she said, "You'd better start looking for a wife for Jonkers." And I swear my heart turned to ice. Just like that.

1 October

Janoo says I talk like an uneducated and that I'm very supercilious and that what happened to Kulchoo was just an accident and had nothing to do with Aunty Pussy's promise or Jonkers' wife or anyone. But I damn care. Janoo can go on speaking like the bore from Oxford that he is (I think so, they are called Oxens *na*—people with passes from Oxford). But I have very good sick-sense like that. Just like I knew Benazir was going to be killed the day before she was killed, just like that I know deep inside my heart that Aunty Pussy is responsible for Kulchoo's con-cushion. And that if I don't get Jonkers married by the end of the year, God knows what will happen to my baby.

Kulchoo is resting upstairs. I've told him "no reading-sheading, okay?" So he's watching a film on his DVD. Something called *Black Hawk Down*. I think so it's a nature documentary. So serious my baby is. Between you, me, and the four walls, he's becoming a little bit bore like his father, always watching documentaries about global warning and energy crisis and other bore, bore things like that. But thanks God, he's at home.

Every day threats are coming to his school from beardo-weirdos saying they will bomb it. Girls schools' headteachers

10

are being threated night and day that they'll burn down their buildings and throw acid in the girls' faces because their uniform is unIslamic. Just look at them! What can be more Islamic than a shirt that comes down to your ankles and a *shulloo* that has more cloth in it than a three-seater sofa? Cracks. Everyone is saying it's only a matter of time before the beardo-weirdos make schools shut down forever like they did in Swat and Kabul. Sunny was saying at the coffee party that they *tau* are thinking of sending their youngest son to a boarding school in England. Her youngest is one year senior to Kulchoo at school and a real stuppid. He has two, two tuitions in every subject, and even then just manages to scrap through. Sunny was boasting about some top school called Eaten just on the outer-skirts of London whose fees are more than Pakistan's GDB. Show-offer.

2 October

Before I could go see Aunty Pussy, guess who came calling? Jonkers. I was lounging in my lounge, flickering through my fave magazine, *Good Times*—there was a photo of Sunny taken at Lucky Rice-*wallahs'* anniversary party but luckily her eyes were shut and her mouth open as if she was asleep talking— when the bearer came in and said that my cousin Jonkers was here.

Last thing I wanted to see was Jonkers. Don't think I'm not family-minded. Or that I don't like Jonkers. We grew up together, after all. He was always small and skinny and had asthma and used to wheeze like a broken accordion. Auntie Pussy wouldn't let him play with the boys because she said he was too weak. So instead he played with me. Ludo and bedminton and dolls and house-house also. In house-house I was always the *begum sahiba* and he was the driver. "Drive straight to beauty parlour, driver," I'd say to him. "Yes, *Begum Sahiba,*" he'd say. So cute he was then with his long white socks, his ironed shorts, and his hair combed nicely to one side.

But when we became teenagers we grew apart. I got more into my friends and he got more bore. Became all studious

and all and then went away to become a countant in England—
I think so in a place called Hull or Dull or something. Meanwhiles I got married. I'd already had Kulchoo by the time he
came back with his a countancy. Jonkers started helping his
father, Uncle Kaukab. Uncle Kaukab has a small business
exporting bed-sheets and towels-showels and, just between
you, me, and the four walls, a bigger business managing all
the property that he'd collected when he was chief of central
board of revenew back in the '8os. God was very kind to them
then. He put a lot in their way. And as Aunty Pussy's always
said, "God helps those who help themselves." So Aunty Pussy
and Uncle Kaukab helped themselves nicely to whatever came
their way—houses, plots, cars, and so on and so fourth.

They lost some when Musharraf's guvmunt did its little a
countability drama in the begining. Uncle Kaukab panicked
and sold some of his houses quickly and lost money on them.
Then Aunty Pussy investigated whatever money he got from
the sale in her cousin's (from her father's side) motel in Ontario
and the cousin sold the motel and ran off with everything. So
they're not as well off as before but still not poor, God forbid.

Aunty Pussy wanted Jonkers to make a big marriage, *na*,
to nice, rich, fair, beautiful type from an old family. At first,
tau, she didn't like any girl. Whoever she saw wasn't rich enough
or beautiful enough or fair enough or old family enough. So
it was a real shock to her when she discovered that Jonkers
was secretly dating low-class, hungry-naked types.

There was that receptionist we called Typhoon (she used
to say phoon instead of phone) whom Aunty Pussy had to pay

off. Then there was another polyester number with underarm sweat stains and chipped nail polish, who worked in a furniture showroom, but who thanks God Jonkers himself caught in the muscular embrace of the security-*wallah*. In between also there was a cheap-type hairdresser. Actually not even proper hairdresser, she was just a blow-dryer. Her name was Akeela and Mummy and I called her Akela the loan wolf—from *Jungle Book*, which was my best film until *Kuch Kuch Hota Hai*. And then last year Jonkers arrived home with Miss Shumaila, his secretary, with whom he'd already done secret marriage in a mosque.

And if we thought Akela was bad, Shumaila was ten times worst. So pushy and hungry and low-class. Wore tight polyester shirts and frosted maroon lipstick and had big busts and wobbly hips that juggled as she walked. And even more worst she had a meaty, furry smell about her as if a wild animal, like a female monkey or fox or something, had entered the room. Jonkers, of course, was like her lapdog, following in her meaty trail with his tongue hanging out. Honestly, all men are cracked. She stayed with him for four months, lying about in her unmade double bed in her air-conditioned room all day, eating nine, nine meals in one sitting, ordering the servants like they were her own and doing twenty-four-hour arguing with Aunty Pussy. Of course, after she'd had her little holiday, she ran off. Took a good clunk of Aunty Pussy's jewellery and Jonkers' brand-new Toyota Corolla and ran off in the dead of night with some low-class cheapster man like herself. Good radiance, I thought. Last month, thanks God, die-vorce came through.

Of course, Aunty Pussy *tau* can't stop crowing about how she knew from first second that Shumaila was bad news. Day and night she is telling Jonkers, "See! See! Bring two-*paisa*, thieving sluts into an honest, decent home and this is what happens!"

After Shumaila left, Jonkers became so quiet and sad that I don't know what to say to him any more. Sometimes I wonder if he is same Jonkers who used to play bedminton with me and let me win all the points. Maybe he also wonders if I'm still the same me?

Just as I was about to tell the bearer to tell him that I was out, I heard Jonkers' shy little cough and there he was behind my sofa.

"*Haw, Jonkers!*" I squealed. "What a lovely surprise!"

"Hello, Apa," he said quietly. I wish he wouldn't call me Apa. I know I'm his sort of elder sister but he's only three years younger than me even though he looks ten years elder with his bald head, skinny little neck and big, square General-Zia-type glasses.

"May I?" he asked, looking at the sofa.

"Jonkers, *yaar*, don't be formal."

He twitched up his neatly pressed khaki trousers over his knees and sat down.

"I hear, Apa—"

"Don't call me Apa, okay? People will think I'm fifty if I'm *your* elder sister."

"Sorry. My mother tells me you're going to help her find a wife for me?"

"Something like."

"But the sort of girls my mother is after want Porsche-driving, stinking-rich hunks, not losers like me."

"*Haw*, Jonkers, how you can say that? After all, *mashallah*, you have everything—name, house, property."

"I know you all thought Shumaila was downmarket, but you know something? She actually *liked* me."

"If she liked you so much why did she run away then, *haan*?"

"Because everyone looked down on her and my mother made her life hell."

"I'm sorry, Jonkers," I said, "but she was *tau* a total no-no. Couldn't even speak English properly and ate her omlette with a spoon and had pointed toenails. And those tight, tight shirts and loose, loose morals. And no deodorant also. No, I'm sorry. She was just after your money. Look at the way she cleaned you out. And that also in four months only." As soon as I said it I saw Jonkers' face fall down. I felt bad, so I said, "I'm not saying she didn't like you. Don't get me wrong, *haan*? But honestly, she wasn't suitable. There was too much of difference in you both."

"Aren't the two of you different?"

"Who two? Me and Janoo? Of course we are. He is serious and I am fun. I have friends and he doesn't. I am sophisty, socialist-type and he is bore, serious-type. I like fashion and gossip and parties and all he, poor thing, knows about is world affairs and crops and his bore charity school that he runs in his village. But at least we know the same people and have the same sort of baggrounds. Okay, he's landed and I'm not but if he went to Aitchison College, I went to Kinnaird College.

And okay, I spent more time gossiping and getting my eyebrows threaded by my friends in the front lawn than going to bore lectures at college, but at least I went to same place as his sisters for my BA so you know, we are from same bagground. And that's what matters, Jonkers. Not what you like and don't like, not what you do and don't do but where you're from. Can you say that about you and Shumaila? That you were from same sort of baggrounds?"

Jonkers shook his head. And then he said, with a sloppy-type, sad smile, "She used to make me feel alive. I'd take her for a spin in the car and she'd lower the window right down and sing along with Bollywood songs on the radio at the top of her voice. 'It's the Time to Disco' from *Main Hoon Na* was her all-time favourite."

"No, stupid. It's from *Kal Ho Naa Ho* with Preety Zinda and Shahrukh and Saif."

"And she loved Kit Kat. And she wasn't insect-thin and she didn't turn up her nose at clothes without labels and she didn't moan about the servants or the air conditioning and she could cook. She made the best *biryani*. Mummy said it just proved she was servant class."

I felt sorry for him and also a little bit guilty, but why I don't know, because it wasn't me who pushed her out. Also a small voice inside my heart said that a fat diamond ring, two pairs of hairloom earrings, a big gold necklace, and a brand new Toyota salon car isn't too bad for four months of Kit Kat eating and driving up and down the canal road singing "It's the Time to Disco."

So I gritted my teeth and asked him if he wanted her back. Seeing he missed her and her *biryani*. But inside I was praying that he would say no because she *did* have pointy toenails, you know. And she said "tap" instead of "type" and "toash" instead of toast. A total uneducated she was. And also, I'm sorry to say, low-class.

He shook his head. Thanks God.

"She got remarried a couple of weeks ago. To the manager of a *tandoori* restaurant in Dubai. She *so* wanted to visit Dubai. I was going to take her for her birthday. But she ran away the week before."

"Look at the bright sides. At least you saved on the tickets."

He took out his handkerchief and wiped his glasses. Then he asked me such a stuppid-type question.

"Apa, are you happy? Happily married, I mean?"

"*Haw*, crack," I laughed. "What cracked things you ask!"

"I'm serious, Apa. Are you happily married?"

"Don't call me Apa."

"Sorry. Are you?"

"Honestly, Jonkers!" I said. I mean what stuppid question, no? *Am I happily married?* What does he mean? Can't he see? Is he blind or something? By grace of Allah, I have a husband, a child, a big house, servants, social life, status, cars, cupboards full of designer *joras* and jewellery, and so on and so fourth. Everyone is always saying what a nice life I have. What else is happiness, *haan*? Stuppid.

So I waved my arms around my nice cluttered-type lounge, at the walls full of paintings and vases full of flowers and

Janoo's bursting bookcases and Kulchoo's tittering stacks of
DVDs and my piles of *Good Times* and *Vogue* and the huge
colour photo taken by Lahore's best photographer, Zaidi, of me
and Janoo and Kulchoo when he was a baby and before that
of me and Janoo as new weds and I said, "Look at all this.
See? It's a full house. With family and servants and comings
and goings and phones ringing and droppings in of guests and
everyone lively and busy and everything. I have a full house,
Jonkers, a full house."

Jonkers stared at the carpet and nodded and went on
nodding as if the carpet was asking him questions. Then he
coughed, put his glasses on and said, "So you recommend an
arranged marriage?"

"What else?"

"But what about love?"

"*Haw*, who says you can't have both together? Take me
only. I didn't know Janoo at all before we got engaged but I
fell in love as soon as my engagement was announced. Maybe
you're not knowing all this, Jonkers, because you were in Dull
then—"

"Hull," he said, "not Dull."

"What? Oh yes. Du—, I mean, Hull. But Janoo was in love
with an English girl, a real little *memsaab* with blue eyes and
yellow hair, who'd been with him in Oxford. He wanted to
marry her. Stuppid, he thought she'd come and settle in
Sharkpur with him and go ooh and aah over the sunset and
the fields and do bore NGO-type things with him like building
clinics and toilets and things for his precious villagers. But

when she came and visited and saw Sharkpur with its mud houses and big black cows and little black people and the Old Bag, I mean, his mother and all, she told him then and there only that if he wanted to marry her, he'd have to move to London, because no way was she going to live in that hole-hell. She even turned up her nose at Lahore. Imagine! Her ears and graces! So, anyways after she left, for a year or two Janoo went mooning about the place. Very depressed and all he was. But then Janoo's older sister, Cobra—"

"You mean Kubra, Apa?"

"Cobra is my little pet name for her. Because she speaks with split tongue. Anyways, Cobra then suggested me because I was one of the most illegible girls of my year at Kinnaird College, *na*. And so it was done. And the minute our engagement was announced, I fell in love. Didn't think I should fall in love before because what if engagement didn't take place? Then I would become a laughing stop. One has to think of oneself also, *na*. But you wait and see. It will be exact same for you."

"For a thirty-seven-year-old heap of soiled goods like me?"

"Men are never soiled, Jonkers, only women."

He folded his hanky neatly and replaced it in his shirt pocket.

"But I'm not rich. I make a small living running my business and looking after my father's property but I'm not, you know, stinking-rich. I'm also not a double for George Clooney and—"

"And also your clothes, they are not right."

He looked down at his shirt that was buttoned all the way up to his chin.

"My clothes?"

"They are not, you know, fashiony."

"They're not?"

"They make you look like a countant."

"But I *am* one."

"Okay, okay, forget."

"Thing is, I don't know what to say to these society girls. They look snooty and bored. They find me dull and to them, I probably *am* dull. That was the thing with Shumi. Talking to her was so easy . . ."

"At least you can change your glasses. Best is, get your eyes lasered. It's become very cheap. Even the poors, like teachers and all are doing laser nowdays."

"She was chatty and friendly and *genuinely* interested in me."

I'd forgotten he's so stuppid. It's total time-waste to tell him about make-outs like they do on TV where they take really ugly, old people and in one hour flat make them young and beautiful. Jonkers is so behind everything. And then he asked me if I would go along with Aunty Pussy when she went girl-hunting and made sure she didn't go chasing the wrong types. He told me to stare her in the right direction. So I told him that she's not a donkey and that I wasn't sitting on her back with a stick to make her go this way and that way, like I wanted.

"I know, I know," he said. "But she listens to you more than she does to me. She thinks I'm an idiot. And that my views don't matter. After Shumaila left the way she did, she feels she can say whatever she wants to me. I can't open my mouth without her jumping down my throat. Please go and see the girls with her."

"And then?"

"Then just tell her the ones you think are unsuitable."

"But what type of girl do you want, Jonkers? I don't know that even." Well I know he likes the cheapster Typhoon and Shumaila types but he'd better not say that to me. Or I'll slap him.

"I don't want a glamour puss. Nor a spoilt, rich doll. Just someone who is friendly and kind and speaks to people right and is normal, I guess."

"So you want plain, quiet, mediocre-type."

"I want someone who's easy to live with."

"*Uff Allah!* It's not like girls are exams, Jonkers. Hard or easy. Girls are girls. Some are nice and some are not so nice because they are not from good baggrounds. That's all."

He asked me what a good bagground was and I said it was when they had same-to-same money as you and knew the same people and went to same places. Stuppid. Doesn't even know that much. God knows what they taught him in Dull. But then I reminded myself that he may look like a loser but one thing Jonkers has never done is bitch about that bitch Shumaila. Even after she made him into a joke in front of all of Lahore by running off with her *tandoor-wallah*, he never said one word against her. It would have been so easy. Everyone would believe him because he's one of us and she isn't. And here *tau* men say such dirty, filthy things about girls who haven't even done anything to them and they ruin their reputations just like that and Jonkers didn't even say a word. Not a single thing. Not even to me. His Apa.

"Okay, okay," I sighed, "I'll go and see your prospectus brides. But one thing you tell your mother. She's not to make any wishes inside her head without telling me first, okay? Otherwise I'm not coming."

"What wishes? I don't follow."

"Just tell her like I said. *She'll* follow."

4 *October*

So Aunty Pussy came round with Mummy in toe and brought
lemon tarts from Punjab Club and a big buffet of roses for me
and a get-well present for Kulchoo who'd already got well and
gone to school. I think so she was trying to do make up with
me. I wanted to tell her what she'd done was mean, mean,
mean and how could she think such bad things for her own
cousin's daughter's son like that but then I caught Mummy's
eye and she gave a small shake of her head and so I let buygones
be buygones. Because I'm like that only.

We sat in the sitting room and made plans. Over samosas and
lemon tarts Aunty Pussy said that she still gives thousand, thousand thanks to Allah that He saved her poor innocent Jonkers
from that slutty secretary, that poisonous she-snake, Miss Shumaila.
Inside my heart I thought it would have been nicer if He could
have saved the diamond ring, hairloom earrings, one necklace,
and a Toyota salon car also. But something's better than nothing.
And besides you can't expect so much from Someone who's so busy.

"I still can't see what Jonkers saw in her," said Mummy.

"Oh, Malika," said Aunty Pussy, flinging down her napkin.
"She was making sex appeals to him. Of the dirty kind. Girls
like that have no pride, you know, no shame."

24

We were all quiet after that. I think so we were all imagining what the sex appeals must have been like. I didn't say, but I must say I was a bit shocked that Aunty Pussy and Mummy should be thinking such dirty thoughts. At their age. When they should be thinking of God and graves. Just look at them!

Mummy suggested that Aunty Pussy should make a shopping list of all the most illegible girls of Lahore and then do some window-shopping before making a shortlist and final purchase.

"If we have to go to each and every one's house, Mummy, and see them one by one that will take till Doomday," I said. "Remember Jonkers has to be married by New Year. Better is to go somewhere we can see five, six together. In bunches."

"We could go and park outside Kinnaird College and have a good look at forty, fifty of them as they come out from the college gates," said Aunty Pussy.

I said no. One, because after the threats from the beardo-weirdos there is so much of barb-wire and security check posts outside Kinnaird that you can't get to the gates and two, I remember from my time at Kinnaird how much fun we used to make of mothers who did like that. Desperate Aunties, we called them.

And Mummy said that if we did that we could also find ourselves parking up the wrong tree. Nowdays lot of girls were coming to Kinnaird whose fathers were shopkeepers from Brandeth Road selling toilets and taps and that Kinnaird was not like the Kinnaird of olden times when I was there and when only girls from good baggrounds came.

I told Mummy my time was not olden times, *ji. Hers* was.

"What about a wedding?" said Aunty Pussy. "Can't we go

to a wedding where we can see nice stacks of them together? There must be some big wedding coming?"

And then I remembered the card that I'd got from Shabnam Butt, wife of Retired General Khayam Butt, who has become Lahore's biggest, richest property developer. Their girl is marrying Talwar Khan's boy.

"Which Talwar Khan?" asked Mummy.

"Oh Malika, what's happened to you?" said Aunty Pussy. "Talwar Khan the politician, *bhai*. Who was on Musharraf's cabinet and also was on Nawaz Shareef's before and is now the PM's right-hand man."

"Lots of good girls will come to that wedding," said Mummy.

"All of Lahore will be there," said Aunty Pussy happily.

"All except Janoo. He's already told me flat that he's not going," I said. "He says he doesn't like corrupt, crooked types like that. Anyways, you know how bore he is. Big, big weddings are not his scene. So you two can come with me. I think so, you should bring Jonkers, so he can also see."

But the wedding was still many days away and Aunty Pussy said she couldn't let even a day pass doing nothing for her poor, sad Jonky and so I must arrange some viewing in between. I said I'd see. But inside I wanted to tell her to arrange it herself for her poor sad Jonky if she was in so much of a hurry. I'm not some, God forbid, Madam from Diamond Market who can produce ten, ten girls at the slick of a finger. But I didn't say because Aunty Pussy is a bit touchy-type, you know, and I didn't want anything else to happen to my Kulchoo.

6 October

Yesterday was my kitty day. Kitty, by the way, is *not* a cat. Kitty is socialist way of saving money. We have a group of ten friends, very reclusive and all because we don't just invite anyone to join our kitty, you know. They all have to be nice, rich girls from good baggrounds like ourselves. So we get together every month at one member's house for lunch and each of us contributes ten thousand rupees to the kitty and every month we take turns for one person to take whole lot. And it goes on like this for ten months until everyone's taken a *lakh* of rupees and then we start all over again.

Janoo says he doesn't see the point, because if I was to stuff ten thousand into a piggy bank for ten months I'd still have a hundred thousand at the end. Why to go through all the rig-my-roll of taking turns and keeping count and meeting for lunch and things? I told him that he was a hippo-crit because he was all praise for my maid Jameela who, when she was saving to buy a TV, put money into a committee. (The poors call kittys committees, *na*, which they pronounce "cummaytee" in typical illitred non-English-speaking, *desi* way.) Janoo said that was because Jameela didn't have a bank account nor any investment chances like all the rich *begums* in my

27

group. Nor could she put the money in a jar at home because her no-good brothers would help themselves to her savings. What was a smart move for Jameela was a bloody stuppid waste of time for me. And instead of doing time-waste at kitty parties, I should be helping Jameela open a bank account or something useful like teaching English to the girls in his charity school in Sharkpur. I told him flat I'd rather die than go to shitty Sharkpur with its dirty cow smells and its filthy fields and in any case our kitty wasn't about money. We were least bothered about money. It was just a chance to meet up and do *gup-shup* but I couldn't expect an antisocialist like Janoo to understand importance of chit-chat in a thousand years.

Anyways, the kitty lunch was at Baby's house this time. So me and Mulloo and Maha and Faiza and Sunny and the others, we all got there and sat around doing *gup-shup* from here and there and waiting for Nina when Baby's bearer came in with a note that had been delivered by Nina's driver saying that to please return her eighty thou right now, ten thou for every month that she'd contributed without getting anything in return so far, because she was no longer part of our group and that she'd joined Natasha's kitty instead. And to please send the money right now with the driver. Natasha's husband's just landed a fat guvmunt contract *na* to rebuild schools in the Frontier that the Talibans burnt and we all know what *that* means and besides, and even more importantly, in Natasha's kitty group is also the Army Chief's best friend's wife's sister.

Look at Nina. What a money-minded, snake-in-the-grass, back-stabber. And asking for her money back. What cheeks.

So all the girls got angry and said that why should they give and if Nina wanted her money back she should come back and do the two months remaining properly and wait her turn like everyone else. So they sent her a text saying all that and she texted back saying that she will tell to the Army Chief's best friend's wife's sister and when that happens we shouldn't say that she hadn't said.

So then everyone got after Mulloo and said if anyone should give the money back it should be Mulloo because she introduced Nina to the group. And Mulloo started shouting that why should she and while all of this was going on, Baby took me aside and asked if my aunt was still looking for a girl and I said maybe and she said her niece, Tanya, was foreign-returned and very nice and all and that her sister Zeenat was looking for nice foreign-returned boy and that don't worry money wasn't a consideration and that I should tell to my aunt and let her, Baby, know the next day.

7 October

"Zeenat Kuraishi?" shrieked Aunty Pussy down the phone. "Zeenat Kuraishi of New Dawn School Syndicate? But she's worth *crores* and *crores*. She has schools in every city. At least forty thousand children go to her schools. She makes more than all those sugar mill-*wallahs* and those steel factory owners. The girl will inherit so much, so much that Jonkers won't need to lift a finger ever again." And then she started asking me about the girl.

I told her I hadn't even slapped eyes on her. All I knew was that she was foreign-educated and that her parents were not after money and that Zeenat had asked us for dinner the next night and that we mustn't say anything to the girl because she would hit the ceiling if she knew we were there to check her out. These foreign-educated types are a bit funny that way, *na*. They want everything in life to be their own choice. Aunty Pussy said she always knew her Jonkers would make a match made in heaven and that this was God's way of making up to them for that two-*paisa* piece, Miss Shumaila. And hanging me up, she rushed off to tell Jonkers and to get her hair died and set for tomorrow.

But Mummy was a little bit more precautious.

30

"Zeenat got married at least fifteen years after me," she said. "So her daughter must be in her early to mid twenties. The girl is rich, young, and foreign-educated. Why would she want to have an arranged marriage with an older man who's been married before, isn't half as rich as her and let's face it, darling, is no Carry Grant either?"

"That's what I'm wondering also. But Mummy, just think, if the marriage does happen, how fantastic the wedding will be and how expensive the presents from the girl's side will be to all of us and how heavy our name will become in the world. Everyone will want me in their kitty group. Natasha will *tau* come on her knees."

Jonkers was also a little bit septic about it.

"I don't get it," he said.

"What's to get, *yaar*?" I said.

"Why would a girl like that from that sort of liberal family be up for an arranged marriage?"

"All I know, Jonkers, is that she is and if I were you I'd just think of how nice it would be to have a nice young rich wife and not take out faults in her."

"But even our backgrounds, which you put so much store by, don't match. She's far richer than me."

"Oho, Jonkers you don't understand anything! Baggrounds don't match when the other person's less than yours. They match perfectly when they are richer than you. Okay, I'll admit it is always better when girl is poorer than boy because that way she always looks up to him but don't worry about it, *yaar*. Just like your name will become hers once you get married, her bagground will also become yours. Life's all about give and take, *na*. Let others give and you take."

"I don't know if she'll be my type. I bet she's spoilt and wilful."

"Now don't be bore, Jonkers."

Of course we didn't tell Janoo anything. Because if he'd known he'd never have come in a million years to Zeenat's house. He thinks we should just let Jonkers find his own wife. What does it matter if she's a secretary or poor relation, as long as he's happy? I told you, *na*, that Janoo is crack.

"What do *you* know about what makes people happy?" I asked him after he'd been banging on and on about letting Jonkers find his own happiness.

"Indeed. What do I know about marital happiness?" he said with a twisted-type smile.

So anyways, we told him it's just a dinner and because he admires Zeenat's business brain, even though he thinks Shaukat, her husband, is a time-waste, he agreed. So we're going to check out bride number one.

9 October

"Now *this* is what I call a driveaway!" sighed Aunty Pussy as the gates swung open and we drove into Zeenat's property.

The drive was like an aeroplane's runaway. I swear three trucks could drive side by side for five hundred yards till they reached the porch. Along the way were parked Mercs, and BNWs, and big, big Range Rovers and all the drivers were in uniform with caps like in Hollywood films.

The house was huge. Huger than huge. Three storeys high and so much of glass and steel, that don't even ask. The garden was all land-escaped with palms and fountains and flowering shrubs and not even ordinary shrubs like *motia* or *chambeli* but strange, erotic ones from foreign countries.

The bearers were dressed in starched white *shalwar kurtas* with black velvet caps. I decided there and then that when I got home, I'd also put all my servants in black velvet caps. The sitting room was totally fab. Marble floors. White leather sofas with steel arms. Glass tables. Palm trees. And on the walls everywhere, Art. Big, big Art. All modern, modern, trendy, trendy. And statues also. With twisted noses and hands like frying pans. Reminded me of Janoo's sisters, Psycho and Cobra.

There were three split-unit air conditioners in the sitting

33

room. Three. Each costing forty thou. I know because I just put a new one into Kulchoo's room. If there are thirty rooms in the house you can do calculations for yourself—I can't because I failed in Maths in Class 7 at the Convent of Jesus and Mary—how many ACs they have like that. And also how many generators they need to run them. And how much of diesel each generator drinks. And how much it costs to buy that much of diesel. I told you, *na*, Zeenat is stinking rich.

Aunty Pussy's head was snivelling around like an owl's. Every now and again she'd budge me in the ribs and say, "Look at this, look at that." Like a total villager, I'm sorry to say. Jonkers was fiddling with his tie and kept clearing his throat every two minutes. So embarrassing, honestly. Thanks God, Janoo wasn't being too over. In fact, he looked like he was least bothered.

"Welcome, welcome!" said Zeenat. She must be in her fifties but she looks like she's in her late thirties. Max. Forehead smooth. Cheeks smooth. Neck smooth. Hair streaked toffee and chocolate. (Mulloo says she lives in Bathing Beauties Spa on Jail Road where she takes buttocks injections on her forehead like other people take vitamin pills.) She had diamond solitaires big as rupee coins in her ears. And another as big as a ping-pong ball on her finger. Otherwise plain *shalwar kameez* in green raw silk. Her husband, Shaukat, looked like his own photo negative—white hair, dark skin. Big paunch. Bags—no, suitcases—under his eyes. A carpet of grey, curly chest hairs springing from his shirt that had not one, not two, but three buttons open. Cheapster. He was scrawled in an armchair. Didn't even bother to get up for us. Just raised his glass in our direction and went on chatting to a couple sitting on the sofa opposite.

"You know Zafar and Shehla?" said Zeenat. Apparently they live in Swizzerland where Zafar works for a bank called Golden Sacks. Shehla was in cheetah print, which is a little bit last year, but carrying fab Gucci bag. I wished Aunty Pussy hadn't worn her purple and gold Benarsi sari and her gold necklace. She looked so over. *Chalo* thanks God at least I was properly turned on in my cream Manish Arora outfit with my coffee-coloured Jimmy Choose and my Channel bag.

And then there was Baby and her husband Jammy (his real name's Jamal). Poor Baby, she's like Zeenat's poor rellie. Always hanging about quietly and saying "Yes Zeenie Apa, no Zeenie Apa." And Jammy not speaking until spoken to.

Anyways Aunty Pussy was gushing at Zeenat about her lovely house, her lovely garden, her lovely art, her lovely sofas.

"You forgot her lovely husband," Shaukat called out.

"Oh shush," laughed Zeenat. "You mustn't mind Shaukat. He loves to shock."

"Not just shock, shock and awe," and he laughed in a snarling-type way. I think so, he's jealous that his wife is better known than him. Mulloo says when they married, he was the rich one because he had lands. But he sold his lands to play golf in Singapore and do gambling in Monty Carlo. Now he just lives off her.

We all sat down on the leather sofas. Zeenat, I noticed, sat next to Jonkers who was still gulping and swallowing like a goldfish.

"So as I was saying," said Shaukat in a loud voice, "all these bombs, these are not the work of the fundos."

"Why not?" asked Janoo.

"Because," said Shaukat, "the Talibans were all more-ons, who couldn't even do two plus two. They were even more stuppider than *him*," he said, pointing to his bearer who was serving Janoo a drink. Janoo's eyes narrowed into slips like they do when he's about to blow up. Inside I thought to myself, please God don't let Janoo throw a fit now. The bearer carried on serving quietly but when he left the room Zeenat told Shaukat sharply to watch it because times were bad and last thing she wanted was to be murdered in her own home. Aunty Pussy said no, no, you couldn't trust servants these days and she *tau* even kept her sugar and rice under lock and key. And then Janoo said that if it wasn't the Talibans doing the bombing, who was it. Shaukat said it was the Americans. Zeenat meanwhiles was trying to ask Jonkers about where he studied.

"I was at Hull," said Jonkers. "Then I worked for Coopers in London for two years before coming back."

"Did very well, *mashallah*," said Aunty Pussy. "Came top."

"Why?" asked Janoo.

"Because he's very clever, by grace of God. And hard-working also," smiled Aunty Pussy.

"Actually, don't tell me. Let me guess. It's to destabilize Pakistan and break it up into little pieces and then move in and take our nuclear weapons."

I hate when Janoo becomes like this. He gets into so many arguments. He's quarrelled with Tony, with Akbar, with everybody.

"And now?" asked Zeenat from Jonkers.

"I run a small business exporting textiles."

"You know, towels and tablecloths and napkins. He's about to get into bed-sheets now," added Aunty Pussy. "And we have another family business besides."

"Exactly! That's what the Americans want. They can't stand the idea of an Islamic bomb. They're taking orders from Israel."

"And the other family business is—?" asked Zeenat.

"Er, a bit of real state."

"Jesus! I can't believe my ears!" said Janoo.

Thanks God just then the drawing-room door was flung open and a girl thumped into the room. She was barefooted with shoulder-long, frizzy hair, like a cloud of mosquitoes buzzing round her head. She was wearing jeans that just covered her bottom and a crumbled T-shirt on top that showed a tire of meat between hem of shirt and waste of jeans. And no make-up also.

"Mom, Dad, have you seen my Blackberry?"

"Come, darling," said Zeenat. "Come and meet everyone. I was about to send for you. Jehangir, this is our daughter Tanya. She graduated from Smith a year ago. She was in New York for a short while and now she's home, to help me out a bit. Isn't that right, sweetie?"

"Have you seen my Blackberry?" the girl repeated without so much as giving Jonkers a single glance. Or a smile to anyone.

I looked at Aunty Pussy. Her mouth was hanging open like a labradog's. I quickly budged her in the ribs with my elbow.

"How the hell should I know where your Blackberry is?" asked Shaukat. "Am I its keeper?"

Tanya rolled her eyes but just then one of the bearers brought it to her on a silver tray. He said she'd left it in the pantry.

"You're a star, Nazeer," she said to him and winked. A wink! At a bearer! Honestly, these foreign-educated types are also too much. Next they'll be sitting down to eat with servants.

Zeenat managed to seat Tanya next to Jonkers but Tanya might as well have been sitting next to a dustbin. So much attention she gave to him. The whole time she just texted on her phone and replied with "uh-huhs" to the questions Aunty Pussy kept firing at her. Was she enjoying being home? Uh-huh. Must be nice, no, to be back with her Mummy, Daddy? Uh-huh. Had she seen *Three Idiots*? Uh-huh. She must, it's such a nice film. Uh-huh. At last Aunty Pussy gave up and shut up. But when she thought no one was watching, Aunty Pussy frowned at Jonkers and jerked her head towards Tanya. So Jonkers cleared his throat again and asked Tanya what she'd been doing in America and Tanya said without taking her eyes off the phone, "Partying. Clubbing. Living, basically."

Tanya put her bare feet on the glass table in our faces. The souls of her feet were black, I tell you, *black*. But I think so it must be some latest fashion in New York. I know from the TV channels that Kulchoo watches that some very fashiony people go about with unwashed hair and loose jeans hanging from their hips as if they had a huge soaking pamper inside. They call it "hobo-cheek." I think so this must be that also. But I wonder if it's also "hobo-cheek" to not thread your upper lips, especially if they look like Saddam Hussein's.

Meanwhiles Janoo and Shaukat and Jammy and Zafar had got back to discussing politics and Zafar was saying it was impossible for a Muslim to kill another Muslim. That's why he was sure it wasn't the Talibans who were doing the bombings. Janoo said okay then who did all the killing in the Iraq and Iran war in which a million people died and Zafar said that was *tau* hundred per cent the Americans. And then Jammy said it was the Israelis and I said to Zeenat that her highlights were very nice and who had done them and Shehla asked Tanya if she'd come and stay with them in Swizzerland and she replied, "No offence but Geneva sucks."

Zeenat looked hard at Tanya but Shaukat laughed as if she'd just cracked best joke in the world. I don't think so I like Shaukat. Tanya opened a can of beer, took two huge gulps, and rubbed the back of her hand across her mouth. Jonkers cracked his knuckles and stared at the ceiling and Zeenat and Aunty Pussy gave each other fake smiles.

Then the bearers came and said dinner was ready. Food was a mix-up of local *desi* and western. Green salad and lamb roast and *haleem* and prawns tempura and chicken shashlik and *rogan josh* and *biryani* and the crockery was Herend (I checked) and the glasses were heavy crystal and Tanya piled up her plate and spoke only to the servants. "Water," and "More ice," and "Thanks, *yaar*." Everyone else she ignored. Zeenat kept trying to get her to talk to Jonkers but she ignored them both. The only time she said anything to anyone of us was when Aunty Pussy asked her how she was passing her time in Lahore and Tanya said, "Doing sweet FA."

"You are doing your FA?" asked Aunty Pussy. "But your mother said you'd already done BA?"

And Shaukat hooted with laughter, spraying poor Baby with chewed-up rice and roast. Didn't say sorry even. Even Jonkers' and Janoo's and Zafar's lips twitched but Zeenat scowled at Tanya and said, "Tanya's actually helping me in the admin of my schools."

"Yeah, you wish," Tanya muttered and threw her napkin to the floor and thumped out. Didn't say goodbye even.

10 October

Now you will say I can't even go to the toilet without asking Mulloo first. I swear I don't ask her about anything except society stuff—you know, who's up to what and why and with whom and so on and so fourth. And that's also only because Mulloo is a suppository of all the local goss. You can ask anyone. They will all say it is Mulloo. Because she makes it her business to find out. So if you want the inside story about anyone, ask Mulloo.

So I called her the next morning and after doing full half an hour of innocent-type *gup-shup* to kill her suspicions, I asked her about Tanya.

"What do you think of Zeenat's daughter, Tanya?" I asked super-casually.

"Why?" At once she became a lert, her voice all sharp and pointy like my D&G heels.

"Just like that, Mulloo."

"Is your Aunty thinking of sending *proposal* for her?"

"*Haw*, Mulloo, Aunty Pussy hasn't even heard of Tanya."

"It would be totally useless."

"Why?" and now I became a lert.

"Because she's not like that."

41

"Like what?"

"Bridal type."

"Meaning?" ·

"She is a gay."

"A *gay*? *Haw*, how do you know?"

"You can see for yourself. The upper lips. The clothes. The hair. Besides, everyone knows she was dating this girl—American, even worse, Christian—in New York."

I wanted to say that at least Christians were people of the Book and it wasn't as bad as a Hindu or something but then I didn't, one, because Mulloo would become suspicious if she thought I was taking Tanya's side and two, because I didn't know whether that people of the Book thing applied to gays.

And then Mulloo told me about how Tanya had been living with this girl called Holly or Holy, whatever she was, like husband and wife. In one-bed flat. Imagine. Apparently Nina's sister-in-law's daughter's best friend had been in that all girls' college with them and she says everyone there knew. But I tell you these American girls' colleges, they are also too much. Everyone who goes there becomes a gay. My cousin Sabeena had a daughter who also went to one and she also became that way. Not fully gay. But definitely gayish. When she came back she wouldn't wash her hair or wear deodrant and kept saying things like "Fat is a Femnist Issue." I think so Femnist Issue was their college newspaper. Anyways, thanks God she grew out of it and now she's married with three kids and living with her engineer husband in Jeddah in an *abaya*.

Haan, so where was I? Yes, Tanya. So the American girl,

Holi or Holey or something—honestly why can't they have straight names like Bubble and Sunny and Baby?—she was one year senior and when she finished and left for New York, Tanya also dropped out of college like a lizard from the ceiling, and followed her. And all that year Zeenat kept putting her college fees and also big fat allowance on top, in her bank account and Tanya kept taking it out and spending on Holy in New York and not coming home even for holidays and telling her mother it was because she was too busy studying. Zeenat was going around proudly, saying my daughter is such a turd or nurd or whatever it is they call bookwormy children. Poor Zeenat. Then finally college wrote to Zeenat and asked if her daughter was ever coming back to finish her degree and Zeenat *tau* of course went up the well. She took the first flight to New York and she went straight from airport to the apartment where that leach Holy was living off her hard-earned earnings and she put the bank account into deep freeze and grabbed Tanya by her frizzy hair and dragged her back to Lahore.

At first *tau* Holy kept calling Tanya and saying her heart was breaking and that she'd wait for her till Doomday and Tanya kept screaming at Zeenat that she'd kill herself if she wasn't allowed to be with her true love but Zeenat also didn't budge. Not an inch. Once Holi realized that no more money was coming, she *tau* dropped Tanya like a hot samosa. And now Tanya is sitting in Lahore skulking and texting.

"Zeenat wants to get Tanya hitched, before everyone finds out," said Mulloo. "But no nice-looking, rich boy from good family is going to have her. So she's looking at second-raters now. But a decent, mousy, second-rater who won't run off with her money or throw his affairs in her face. Why are you asking?"

"*Haw*, Mulloo, how suspicious you are, *yaar*. I was asking just like that."

12 October

Look at them! The terrorists attacking the Headquarters of the army itself. So much guts they've got. Janoo says it serves the army right. They were the ones who brought the beardo-weirdos up in the first place, arming them and training them and sending them into India and Afghanistan and God knows where all to do *jihad*. And then saying to Americans, promise by God we don't know where the fundos have gone, while all the time quietly giving them safe heavens in Pakistan. I didn't say to Janoo but isn't it a bit ungrateful of the *jihadis* to turn around and attack the army after everything it's done for them?

But I think so the *jihadis* are angry because of the way the army threw them out of Swat and Dir and all and now army's saying that they're going to go and flush them down in South Waziristan also where they're all hiding. And why? Because Americans are saying that we won't give you any aids otherwise and because of this horrid economic slum that's closed Mulloo's husband Tony's sanitary pads factory and put everyone in so much of depth to the banks, we can't do without American aids *na*. I think so our country is hungry-naked. So that's why we're attacking Waziristan and that's why the fundos are attacking us.

Meanwhiles Obama's been given Noble peace prize and Tony was saying a man who sends drawns every other day to kill innocent Pakistanis, how is he getting peace prize, *haan*? And Janoo said the planes target Al Qaeda leaders and not innocent Pakistanis. And Tony said yes, yes, Al Qaeda-*wallahs* sit there with big, big signs around their necks saying strike here, *haan*? And Janoo said, how else . . . but I stopped listening because (a) their talk was very bore and (b) because thanks God my mobile phone rang just then.

But not so many thanks to God after all, because it was Aunty Pussy eating my head and drinking my blood like she does every day about Jonkers. She wanted me to come over there and then and discuss Tanya Kuraishi with her.

"I am ready to go and put formal proposal on them," she said. "I've taken out my gold bangles, all twenty-four of them from the bank and if they say yes, which they will because we saw how much Zeenat was talking to Jonkers, I'll immediately put all twenty-four of my bangles on Tanya's arm and set the date. What do you think of 1 December? Of course we'll have to ask my fortune-teller woman before I can fix proper date but—"

"Aunty Pussy, please," I said. "Please don't do like this. Wait till tomorrow and then we'll discuss and decide."

"What's to discuss? What's to decide? Girl likes boy, boy likes girl. What's the problem?"

"Jonkers likes Tanya?"

"And why not? She's rich, she comes from good family. Naturally he loves her."

"Listen to me, Aunty. We'll speak tomorrow. Okay?" And before she could say anything else I quickly hanged up on her. Then I took two Panadolls from my bag and swallowed them without water even. I swear, between Aunty Pussy and Janoo, my nerves have shattered.

And if that wasn't enough, when I got home that evening, my maid, Jameela, came into my room and announced that she wanted to have three days off because her mother had died.

"The same mother who died last year also?" I asked her.

She started crying and said that that was actually her aunty, her father's sister, who died last year but she used to call her Baybay because she's married to her son and now it's her real mother who's died. I'm sure she's telling lies. These people always tell lies. They don't know truth from lies. Because they haven't been to good convent schools like us, that's why. But if I don't let her go, she'll probably go off and find another job (I've seen the way Sunny eyes her, like a cat eyes a rat). And if Jameela leaves then not only will I have to find a new wife for Jonkers but a new maid for myself also. *Uff Allah!* I bet even Obama doesn't have so many worries. And at least he's been given the Noble Prize. What have I been given for everything I do for everyone? Nothing!

13 October

"My grandmother used to say that even a dead elephant is worth a fortune," said Aunty Pussy when I told her what Mulloo had said about Tanya. "Whatever she does, whoever she is, at least she can give my Jonky a comfortable life. And you shouldn't listen to gossip. Jealous people say all sorts of things."

"But Aunty Pussy—"

"You remember Sabeena's daughter?" she went on as if I hadn't even spoken. "How she wouldn't use deodrant? Or wash her hair? Look at her now. Happily ironing her husband's shirts in Jeddah. *Happily!* You remember how much I used to faint after my head girl at school, Malika? This is a phase. Everyone goes through it. Tanya will also pass out from it."

I'd taken Mummy along to Aunty Pussy's for hand-holding. Mine, not hers. And thanks God I had because Aunty Pussy *tau* that day was completely impossible. So puffed out with importance, she was almost floating above our heads like a twenty-rupee gas balloon. Inside her mind she was already halfway to the wedding reception. Speaking about Zeenat as if they were old friends and as if the dinner was all her own idea. Just look at her!

"But you weren't living with your head girl like her husband, Pussy," argued Mummy.

"Oh, Malika, you also always insist on looking on the bad side. Leave it now. Everything will be fine."

When I'd told Mummy about Mulloo's report on Tanya, Mummy had straight away asked me if I thought Mulloo was jay (jealous, what else?) that we were about to become related to Zeenat Kuraishi and her *crores*.

"I know it would never occur to you, darling, because I've brought you up nicely but people can mislead out of jealousy, you know."

So I'd told her that I didn't know about the New York bit and the American girl but Tanya's upper lips *tau* I'd seen with my own eyes. And yes, she also didn't wear make-up, not even a line of coal under her eyes. Also, I told Mummy, she wasn't like other young girls because she was least bothered to make good impressions on other people. And she hardly spoke to Zeenat. Or to us. And her father was not so nice, all bitter and nasty. But the house was fab and Zeenat looked desperate. And Mummy said that yes, family was important, very important, but only half your marriage was to the family. The other half was to your husband or wife. I don't know if Mummy was saying this because she was tiny bit jay herself that Aunty Pussy might go up in the world and she might start looking down at us from there or because she really wanted best for Jonkers.

If I am to hold the Holy Koran in my right hand and say the truth, I'd say that when Baby first told me, I got very excited and thought only of myself and how my name would become so big and heavy and how much praise I'd get for arranging the marriage. But when I went to the house and saw how nice it was, I wanted Jonkers to have it but also I didn't want Jonkers to have it. I felt, and I'm only saying this because I'm holding the Holy Koran, that it was too good for Jonkers and it should have gone to someone more deserving. Like me. But then when I saw Tanya, and how she was ignoring him and trying to make him feel small, I thought how dare she treat poor old Jonkers like that? Who does she think she is, *haan*? Mitchell Obama? So really, I don't know what I feel.

"Her bagground is fab," I said. "No one can deny. You didn't see their sitting room, Mummy. Only the paintings were worth three *crores*. And Zeenat's diamond ear-studs, at least five, five carrots each. No, Aunty?"

"And so many servants and all so trained," said Aunty Pussy. "Not once did they lift their eyes and look into ours. That's Zeenat's training. I can tell. She is old-blood."

Just then Aunty Pussy's own servant, the hundred-year-old Ghulam, who's been with her forever, came tottering in with the tea tray. Same thousand-year-old Meakin tea service. Same thousand-year-old broken biscuits. And Aunty Pussy sitting there in her dark sitting room on her faded sofa in her thousand-year-old faded kaftan. I don't know why she's such a miser. The toothless Ghulam handed me a plate but it had some crusty thing stuck up to it. I showed Ghulam and he brought it up to his nose to look.

"Where?" he said, his tongue flapping about in his toothless mouth. "Oh this! This is nothing." And he wet the end of his sleeve with spit and rubbed it off with that. "See, Baby, gone." I told him I wasn't hungry because no way, *baba*, was I going to touch that plate again. Also, I wish he wouldn't call me Baby. He's been calling me that since he first came to work for Aunty Pussy. I've thought of telling him once or twice but then I think, let him. He's known me since I was seven and really, what goes of mine if he calls me Baby? As long as he doesn't do it in front of anyone who matters. I wish that Aunty Pussy would buy him a set of dentures. After all, he's worked for her forever.

While tea was being given, Uncle Kaukab came shuffling in, in his slippers and crumbled *shalwar kameez* and even more crumbled, unshaven face and long, grey hair uncombed and wild-looking.

"Hello, Bhaijan," said Mummy in a loud, cheerful, total-fake voice.

"Hello, Uncle," I also said in a loud, cheerful, total-fake voice.

"Is it breakfast time?" he asked, his watery old eyes staring at the biscuits hungrily.

"No, no, it's tea time," Aunty Pussy said extra loudly.

But Uncle Kaukab hadn't heard. "How are you, child?" he asked me in a shaky voice. "Finished your exams?"

"Sunye!" Aunty Pussy yelled at Uncle Kaukab. She's always called him "Sunye," never Kaukab. I think so in the beginning she called him "Sunye" because she was too shy to use his name. And now she calls him Sunye because maybe he's become deaf. But imagine calling your husband "Listen!"

"Sunye, go to your room at once," ordered Aunty Pussy. "We are doing ladies' talk here."

And then she told Ghulam to take Uncle Kaukab into his room and give him tea there.

Poor Uncle Kaukab! He hasn't been the same since he got that beating, *na*. *Haw*, don't you remember? Ten years ago they rented out one of their many houses in Karachi to this harmless-looking, stammering Urdu-speaking-type in thick glasses who drove a small Alto and had a fat wife and four fat daughters and worked as a clerk in some guvmunt department. Anyways, halfway through, Uncle Kaukab suddenly decided to double the rent. When the harmless-type told him he couldn't pay, Uncle Kaukab gave him notice. When the harmless-type didn't move out, Uncle Kaukab went to Karachi himself and drove up his big car to the tenant's house and threatened and shouted and said if he didn't bring him his money that same night at his house in Clifton, he'd be sorry. Well, he *was* sorry. Uncle Kaukab, not the tenant.

The harmless-type with the thick glasses and the stammer turned out to be related to a political party thug-type boss. That same night the boss's handymen visited Uncle Kaukab in his house in Clifton and since then Uncle Kaukab hasn't been himself.

And Aunty Pussy, she was always the bossy type. You know *na* that she got married very late, almost when she was thirty. She was engaged to this dashing air force officer for seven years and then suddenly he went and married his first cousin, leaving her high and dry. All the half-decent boys of her age had been snapped up long since and she was left with nothing. And then Uncle Kaukab proposed. He was a small basic-type officer in guvmunt service in some unsexy department. And very plain also with his toad face and small, skinny body. And he didn't even own a car. Just a scooter. But Aunty Pussy's parents were desperate and they married her off to him. She begged and pleaded with them but they didn't listen. Mummy says she's never seen anyone cry as much as Aunty Pussy did on her wedding day.

But one day soon after she got married, she told Mummy if I can't be happy, let me at least make myself comfortable. And then Aunty Pussy went to work. She found out who Uncle Kaukab's boss's wife was and started making cakes for her and stitching frocks for her children—she was a very good stitcher—and doing full twenty-four-hour flattery of both husband and wife and guess what? Suddenly Uncle Kaukab got promotion. Same thing happened in his next job. And next job and next job, until Uncle Kaukab became chief of central board of revenew. I shouldn't say because they are family and all, but between you, me, and the four walls, after he became chief of revenew Uncle Kaukab and Aunty Pussy helped themselves with both hands to whatever they could—plots, houses, cars, cash, even things like fridges and phones. Articles came in the papers even about Uncle Kaukab. That's why he panicked when all that a countability drama started.

Aunty Pussy must be so angry now that after all those years of sucking up, and bowing and scrapping, they lost all those houses in their panic. And then on top, Uncle Kaukab had to go and argue with that tenant of his so that now once again she's the only real handler of everything in her family. Between you, me, and the four walls, Uncle Kaukab is *tau* out of it.

"Where were we?" said Aunty Pussy.

"In the Kuraishis' sitting room," I reminded.

"Think it through, Pussy," Mummy said. "Jonkers is your one and only. You want him to have children, no?"

"And why won't he?" demanded Aunty Pussy.

"Because Tanya is a gay."

"Again you are going back to the same thing? I'm telling you she'll get over it. These things are like, like . . . flu and chickenpox and soar throats. Everyone gets them and then they pass. Remember Sabeena's daughter?"

"And how do we know Sabeena's daughter is happy?" said Mummy. "She is living in Jeddah and only yesterday someone told me that Saudi is full of it. Women with women. Because the men have no time for them, the women have—"

"Tanya's not Saudi, all right?" said Aunty Pussy.

"But imagine how everyone will laugh at Jonkers. Knowing his wife is a gay."

"Laugh? They will die of jealousy that he's married to such a rich girl." I always knew Aunty Pussy was greedy but not so much that she was willing to become the laughing stop of the whole city. After all, rep—oho *reputation*—is also something, no?

To be honest, I wouldn't say no to that glass-and-steel house full of erotic plants and split ACs and art-shart but could I live in it with a gay? Even worst, a gay who everyone knew was a gay? And a gay who texted all day and never even looked at me. And had filthy feet with black souls. And winked at servants and dreamed of Christian girls. No, nothing doing. We all have some pride. Even Janoo who never notices anything said the girl was rude beyond believe and had no social graces.

I mean, just look at the way she spoke to her parents. Like they were servants or somethings.

And then Aunty Pussy said, "And besides, Jonkers can have his little secretaries and receptionists on the side. He doesn't have to deny himself just because he's married to Tanya. As long as he does it quietly, Zeenat won't mind. She is a woman of the world, she'll understand. And Jonkers will be happy also. Maybe he can even get Shumaila back and set her up in a little *kothi* in Defence."

"Pussy!" said Mummy. "I knew you were money-minded but in sixty-three years of knowing you I never knew you could be so grabby and low."

"Don't pretend you didn't look at your son-in-law's lands and find out exactly how many acres he had and exactly how much each acre was worth, before you married *her* off," she said jabbling her hand in my direction. "Being all high and mighty with me. Giving me lectures when you are same-to-same underneath."

"Janoo is not a gay, Aunty," I said hotly. "We have Kulchoo to proof it. And the whole city is not laughing at me and calling me mousy-type second-rater just because I am married to Janoo."

"Who is calling my Jonky mousy-type second-rater?" Aunty Pussy yelled.

Mummy and I looked at each other and then without saying another word, we picked up our handbags and got up to go. And then we saw Jonkers standing in the doorway. I don't know for how long he'd been standing there. I hope so he hadn't heard me say "mousy-type second-rater."

"Please sit down," he said quietly to Mummy and me. We looked at each other and we put our handbags down and sat down.

"I want to say this in front of all of you, so there are no misunderstandings later: I do *not* want to marry Tanya. I don't care how much money she has or how well known her mother is. I can't see myself with her. That's the end of it. Now either you are going to tell her mother or I will."

"You see yourself with another Shumaila? *Haan?* Who robs us of our, no, *my*, things and cuts our noses in public and runs away? Is that what you want?" shouted Aunty Pussy.

"That's not what I want," said Jonkers swallowing hard. "But I know that Tanya's not the kind of wife I want either."

"You don't know what type of wife you want. You don't know *anything!*" shrieked Aunty Pussy.

Jonkers shut his eyes for a second but then he opened them again and looking straight at Aunty Pussy said, "I'm sorry but I'm not marrying Tanya."

Suddenly the air seemed to blow out of Aunty Pussy. "Just give it two more days, *beta,*" she said in a pleading voice. "Don't make up your mind in a rush. After all, I'm your mother. I know what's best for you."

"No, Ma. My answer will still be no."

I looked at Jonky. I swear I get a little bit frightened of Aunty Pussy when she gets angry, and here was shy, quiet Jonkers standing up to her. Honestly, he really went up in my steam then.

"So that's settled then, Pussy," Mummy said with a sly smile. "Tanya is out."

14 October

Police has taken out an ad in the papers telling us all to be ware of suicide bombers. They say we should watch out for people who look a bit fattish in their top halfs (suicide vests do nothing for your figure, *na*) and are distracted and loudly saying Arabic prayers and sweating like *tandoor-wallahs*.

So yesterday when Janoo had gone out and Kulchoo, thanks God, had gone for tuition, I was at home watching again my best English film, *Bride and Prejudice*. It's an adoption of an English TV series by a famous English TV writer called Jane Austen. And then Janoo says I never watch anything intellectual. Humph! I was at the part in the film where Ashwariya's younger sister is doing the cobra dance when the bearer came and said that a Kashmiri shawl-*wallah* had come and wanted to show me his stuff.

I got all excited thinking maybe I can buy a new double-coloured *shahtoosh* to make Sunny jay with. Ever since *shahtooshes* got band in India they've become harder to find here also. Apparently they're made from the chin hairs of some rare mountain goat which is getting succinct in India and that's why they've put the ban. Trust the Indians to spoil everyone's fun. Honestly. Anyways, thinking it was my old shawl-*wallah*,

Akhtar, I paused the film and told the bearer to put him in the drawing room.

When I walked in, it wasn't Akhtar at all but a thinnish, youngish man who I'd never seen before, in a *shulloo kurta* and wispy beard and a white cap on his head. But even worst, he was wearing a puffy-type leather jacket. And most worst, he had this suitcase lying beside him. I swear I heard it ticking. My colour immediately flew out of my face. He said his name was Imtiaz and that he was from Islamabad and he'd heard from the shawl-*wallahs'* grape-wine that I was a collector of shawls. And then he reached inside his pocket, took something out, and bent towards his suitcase.

Then I lost it. I told him, I said that I didn't have any money and I hated shawls anyway and I'd never bought a shawl in my life and didn't he know there was an economic slum on and we were defaulters and the banks were after us and he mustn't please for Allah's sake open the suitcase and who'd given him my address and I was a God-fearing Muslim and I had a young son and what would become of him and please have some pity. He looked at me as if I was completely crack. But I didn't care and by this time I think so he was more afraid of me than I was of him because suddenly he picked up his suitcase and ran.

When he was gone I called all the servants—bearer, cook, drivers, maid, sweeper, guards-shards, everyone—and shouted at them for letting people into the house that they didn't know when the sich was so bad and why were they such stuppids and just now only I'd soiled a suicide bomber all by myself.

So they also looked at me as if I was a crack but I damn care. Stuppids!

Later that evening Sunny called and said, "Guess what? I've just bought the most *gorge* double-coloured six-yarder *shahtoosh* from this darling little shawl-*wallah* called Imtiaz. And such a good price he gave me! Two times less than that thief Akhtar. Said he'd heard all about me from other shawl-*wallahs*. Apparently, I am known as Lahore's greatest shawl collector. Wait till you see my new six-yarder. You *tau* will just die!"

16 October

Look at Jameela! Just look at her! She's already a whole day late coming back. And not one word, one excuse, one sorry. Just total silence. I've called her mobile twenty, twenty times. Ring goes, but will she pick up? Never. I think so the minute she sees it's my number she presses busy button. Her village is a thousand miles away at the edge of the world, otherwise I'd send someone to drag her back.

I was complaining to Mummy about her and she said, "I bet you, her mother is fat and well. I bet you she's gone for something else."

"Ever since she's got married—"

"When did she get married?" asked Mummy.

"I think so, three months ago. I gave her fifty thou and gold earrings for her wedding. Since then this has been her third holiday."

"That's it. That's why she's gone. To be with her husband. You know, *na,* darling, these people can't live without You Know What. That's what she's gone for. They're not like us. *We* know there's a time and place for everything. But they don't. Because they are uneducated and they are villagers."

I thought for a second that Janoo was also from a village

but then I remembered that he was not uneducated because he was an Oxen and that's why he knows there is a time and a place for everything. Even for You Know What.

But Mummy's right. I'm sure Jameela's mother is in better health than me even. She's gone for You Know What. Just wait till the madam comes back. The minute she walks in I'm going to throw her out there and then. No questions, no answers. Just "go!" And no matter how she weeps, how much she howls, how much she kisses my feet and begs to stay, I'm going to say, "Leave!" Befooling me like that, after I've done so much for her.

You should have seen her when she first came here. Thin and starving and dressed in rags. A real down-and-out pheasant woman from some lost village God knows where. Muhammad Hussain, our driver, brought her and said, please give her a job because they are eating stones in her village. And now look at her. Plucked eyebrows, bleached face, dressed in all my last-season designer *joras* and fat as a hen. And those earrings I gave her, they alone cost me sixty thou. Wait and see what I'll do to her when she comes back. Liar. User. Faker. Hippocrit. As Mummy says, we should never trust these people. They don't have morals. Because they are uneducated. And not from our baggrounds.

17 October

Honestly the sich is so bad, so bad that don't even ask. No water, no electricity, no security, no schools, and still no wife for Jonkers. Every day bombs bursting everywhere and people dying like flies. Just today the beardo-weirdos attacked that police-training centre inside Lahore. Not some faraway place in the Frontier like Peshawar or Swat, or even not so far away as Rawalpindi, but in *Lahore*. Okay, it was on the outer outer-skirts of Lahore in some God-fortaken place called Manawan or something, but still it was Lahore, *my* city. Apparently, they did the attack in broad daylight. Just came running in, shooting Kalashnikovs and bursting grenades and God knows what, what else. What cheeks, no?

As usuals the stuppid police-*wallahs* didn't realize what was happening at first, and when they finally did, they ran away and hid but when they finally, finally realized they were going to get killed in any case, they at last started shooting back. The fighting went on for three full hours before they were all killed (the terrorists, not the police, thanks God; well one or two policemen were also killed, but mainly non-officer-types whose names even don't come in papers). Just imagine! All this happening inside Lahore. Not fifteen miles from where we live.

I swear I feel frightened myself going to the bazaar in case some mad weirdo arrives and shoots me for buying western food like chips or for wearing western clothes like pop-socks. All the time I'm looking over my shoulder, all the time thinking someone standing behind me in a shop or parked besides me on a bicycle in a traffic jam might blow me up. It's been two full months since I went to Avari Hotel on the Mall to get my facial (the spa there's the best at giving facial, *na*). Ever since the Marriott was bombed last year in Isloo—Islamabad, *yaar*—I've *tau* stopped hotelling. The only thing I used to still go for was my facial. Now I get a girl to come to the house but she's not a thatch on the Avari one. And also she has b.o. Honestly, what the Talibans have put us through! So when people say Americans are behind all this killing-shilling, I say I *tau* use Estee Louder products for my facial. And Estee Louder, as everyone knows, is American. So why would Americans put axe in their own foot by causing all the killing in Pakistan so no one could even leave their houses any more to get Estee Louder facials, *haan*? In any case, who is against facials? Is it Americans? No. Is it Indians? No. Is it Talibans? Yes. Yes. Yes. No one but the Talibans.

At least Lahore isn't as bad as Isloo. There *tau* everyone's under house arrest. So many important foreign types keep coming there, *na*, that guvmunt's shut down everything to protect them. First came Senator Carry, remember the one who lost that election to Bush? Then came the Turkish PM, what's his name, Astrakhan or Ardogan or something (such strange, strange names people have) and then Hilary Clinton came. The guvmunt, as you can imagine, is scared sniff about where Talibans will strike next and fearing a repeat of the Sri Lankan cricket team-*wallah* scene, they've closed down whole of Isloo to protect these important types. I swear you can't take three steps without getting stopped by a police-*wallah* at a check post and being searched in places you didn't even know you had.

Everyone in Isloo is *tau* fed up. I was talking to my friend Sammy who lives in Isloo and runs the art gallery, Sammy's Selections, and she said you can't believe how bore life has become. Hardly any parties-sharties or balls are happening. People are frightened of even leaving their houses. And those few brave ones who do go out to a dinner or GT (Get Togethers, of course) have to leave two hours before they're invited because of all the stoppages along the way at police check posts. Honestly!

God knows what will happen when the wedding season starts properly. And this year *tau*, the whole of it is going to be jam-packed into just November and half of December because after that is Muharram, *na*, when nobody can have a ball, let alone throw a proper seven-event wedding. I think so this is going to be a very bore winter. Sunny and Akbar are going off to Dubai for New Year's Eve and winters holidays because they say Pakistan's going to be so bore. I just mentioned to Janoo that maybe we should also go to Dubai for New Year's and he blew up like a rocket launcher.

"Your country is in flames and all you can think of is partying! Are you off your head?"

I wanted to say I will be if I stay here a moment longer but then I thought, would he listen? Never in a thousand years.

On top of that we have no electricity. Oho, I *know* the whole country has no electricity but I mean *we*, *us*. Our generator has gone *thup* again. I think so the servants must be doing something to it (it's kept by their quarters only, because it is too noisy near the house). It's the second time it's broken down in six months. Other people's keep going and going like Queen Elizabeth of England but not ours. Sunny says she hasn't had to change hers even once since all this "electricity conservation" started two years ago. Who does she think she is? Using words like "electricity conservation" as if electricity was a rare animal like the tiger or the *shahtoosh* goat or something. But come to think of it, electricity is becoming rarer and rarer in Pakistan. But still. She can call it "load shedding" like everyone else does. "Electricity conservation" my shoe!

On TV the guvmunt says that it's all the fault of Musharraf's guvmunt that we have no electricity. They say Musharraf didn't plan ahead. But now this guvmunt is saying they are putting in lots of electricity plants into the ground and that soon electricity is going to start coming non stop through the wires like it used to before all this load shedding started and look how much they are doing for us. But we still have four hours of load shedding in our area. Now we'll have to buy a new generator and this on top of the three thou a day we pay for diesel for it and the electricity bill we get for the few hours we get from main line. I've heard they are also going to do load shedding on gas. Thanks God guvmunt doesn't control air otherwise they would also start doing load shedding on *that*.

And if that's not enough Aunty Pussy called again to ask if I had done anything for her Jonky yet.

I told her, "Aunty Pussy I have other things to do also, okay."

"Like what?"

"Like buying a new generator."

"Kaukab's cousin's son has a dealership in generators. I'll tell him to come to your house and I'll make sure he gives you best price."

So Uncle Kaukab's nephew from Gentle Generators came in the afternoon and he told me which one I should get and then two hours later he sent two men around in a van and they brought the new generator and fixed it up and now we have electricity again. And he knocked up seven thou from the price also. That's why family is so important. Because it keeps its promises. Unlike guvmunts.

And when Janoo came home that evening he asked me what I'd been doing all day and I started telling him about the generator and Aunty Pussy and he cut me off halfway and said I must find some real work to do. And then he switched on his computer and I told him if I hadn't got the generator replaced neither he, nor Kulchoo, nor anyone in this house could have done any "real" work, okay?

18 October

I asked Baby where she and Jammy were going for New Year's. They have Canadian passports, *na*, and can go any place any time. Not like us losers who have green passports and have to apply for visas three, four months from before and then wait in thousand-mile-long cues and answer millions of questions to get them. *If* we get them.

"We're here only," she replied.

"Why don't you go to Toronto? To your flat?" I asked. "It's going to be so bore here, with Muharram and no parties and everything."

"*Toronto?*" she shrieked. "Are you joking? Not even my dead body would go to Toronto for New Year's."

"Why?"

"*Haw*, it's so cold, so cold that your blood freezes the minute you step out of the house. No, no, I'd much rather sit here and be warm and depressed rather than go there and be cold and depressed."

And then she told me all about the trip they made to Toronto in winters when they went and got that crooked Indian lawyer to fix it for them so that they don't have to spend the three years they're supposed to spend there to get nationality.

Apparently you have to go only twice. Once to bribe a lawyer to quietly, quietly break Canadian law and then second time to go and swear some sort of oath to never break Canadian law and to pick up your Canadian passport. So anyways, they went in December. They had to go in their children's holidays, *na*, because they wanted the kids to become Canadians also. They knew it was going to be cold so Baby says she packed lots of shawls and instead of taking pop-socks she bought some woolly-type socks from Al Fatah and took them also. First time since she stopped doing games in Class 9 at the convent that she bought socks. Anyways, they landed up in Toronto in the night and got taken straight from airport to hotel and weren't outside for long enough to feel the cold or see the scenery.

So next morning when they woke up they saw that outside there was so much of snow, so much of snow that don't even ask. The kids got really excited and said they wanted to make a snowman and also Baby, whose passion is Bollywood films, immediately saw herself as Kajol dancing in the snow in a chiffon sari but because she hadn't packed any chiffon saris, she thought she'd be western instead and so she and the kids rushed into a shop in the hotel's downstairs bit and the kids bought knitted hats with pomp-pomps and she bought herself a pair of high-heeled pink suede boots (pink is her favourite colour *na*; you should see her and Jamal's bedroom, it's in five different shades of pink) and a cute little sweater with pink furry bits and she wrapped her shawl around her and they all went out in the snow to take photos.

But the minute they stepped into the snow they couldn't stop stepping. Baby says she went down and down and down until the snow was up to her knees. She swears she couldn't see even the tops of her boots, so much they'd gone down into the snow. Her daughter, Mahnoor, who is a bit of a dwarf, poor thing, she *tau* was snowed in up to her hips. It took them full half hour to cross the road and get to the park they had seen from their hotel window. So anyways when they got there, Baby took the camera out of her pocket and said, "Smile!" and the kids said, "But how?" Their faces were frozen into ice sculptors. Promise by God.

And it gets more worst. Having taken the picture of her kids' frozen faces, Baby tried to put the camera back in her pocket and guess what she found? The camera had got stuck up to her hand. You know like when you take old-fashioned tin ice-tray out of freezer and your fingers get stuck up to it? Just like that. Except that in Pakistan it only happens for two three seconds because usually your kitchen is so hot that ice melts in ten seconds flat but in Toronto if you are not wearing gloves outside in the winters and you touch some metal thing your hand stays there forever. Thanks God Baby had not touched a park railing or something fixed up like that, otherwise can you imagine what would have happened? She would have had to stay there like that till the summers. So Baby then tried to separate the camera and her fingers with her teeth and her lips got stuck up to the camera also. And you know, *na*, that Baby before she went to Canada had had cellulight injected into her lips because they were a bit on the cruel-looking and thin side. And now she got so scared that if she pulled hard on her lips what if all the cellulight came gushing out and ruined her new cute jumper with the pink fur?

And also her children were crying because it had started snowing again and Mahnoor said that she was already up to her waste in it and that in another ten minutes she'd get totally buried and her son said he couldn't feel his toes, his ears, or his nose any more and that he felt as if someone had put a steel headband over his head which they were tightening slowly and why hadn't they left him behind in Lahore to play cricket and do Nintendo and he hated them all, but most of all her, Baby. And Baby with the camera and hands and lips all stuck together was shouting at them to shut up and start moving back towards the hotel but the kids couldn't make head or tale of what she was saying of course because she couldn't really move her lips at all and all the time Baby was also thinking of her two-hundred-dollar pink suede boots buried in the snow.

Finally, one hour later when they got back to the hotel and Baby's fingers and face had melted off the camera and her son had got back his ears and his nose and his toes and her daughter had stopped weeping, they all swore that they'd rather die than go out in the snow again. So for the rest of the month that they were in Toronto they stayed in their hotel room only and watched TV and ate burgers and chips and fought with each other and said how much they hated Canada and how much they loved Lahore and Baby wept over her pink suede boots that had become all hard and grey like a donkey's ears. And inside she cursed the crooked lawyer for calling them there in the winters even though to his face she smiled at him and called him *"bhaijan."* That's why they are not going to Toronto for New Year's. And, thanks God, nor am I. Imagine, *yaar*, what a place. The Canadians must be crack to live there, no?

19 October

Guess who came back today? Madam Jameela! Yes, her. That shameless, selfish, ungrateful, sex-mad liar. Strolled in cold as brass, wearing my three-season-old Kami *jora* with the pink embroidery on green bagground, which had cost me twenty thousand then. New shoes, pink heels if you please. And nail polish on her toes. Face all glowing, hair all shining. *Not* looking as if she'd been *near* a funeral.

"*Assalam aleikum,*" she said.

"Get out," I said.

"Okay," she said.

I was dump-founded. What did she mean, "okay"?

"What do you mean *'okay'*? How dare you say okay?"

"I'm doing like you want. You said go so I said okay."

"After all I've done for you—given you job, given you designer clothes worth I don't know how much, given you earrings worth sixty thou, given you leave every time your mother died—you just come in here and say okay?"

"I don't need your job any more. I'm going to Abu Dhabi."

"*Abu Dhabi?* Don't be stuppid. Who do *you* know in Abu Dhabi?"

72

"I'm going to work for foreigners. They pay three, three, four, four times as much as you all."

"Which foreigners? How do you know foreigners?"

Then she told me. Apparently, her husband's older brother has worked in Abu Dhabi for six years as a driver for these foreigners. She doesn't know where they are from but they don't speak English among themselves and are tall with yellow hair. And they speak nicely, always saying please and if you don't mind. And they are very happy with Jameela's brother-in-law. They've given him TV, DVD, fridge, AC even, and fat pay on top. Now they've moved to a bigger house and they need a maid and a cook and they asked him if he knew anybody suitable and so he asked Jameela and her husband.

"So we're going. Next week. Visas and everything is all done. Tickets also. Just came to pick up my clothes. And to tell you."

That night when Janoo came back from Sharkpur, the minute he walked into the room, I told him it was all his fault. He was the one who was always going on about how smart Jameela was and how hard-working and how ambitious. *He* was the one who gave her so much of *phook* and now look what *he'd* done.

"Abu Dhabi, eh?" he chuckled. "Good for her. I always knew she'd go far."

"Well, she has. All the way to air-conditioned Abu Dhabi where the electricity never goes and bombs never burst and servants speak English. And me? I'm stuck in dirty, filthy Lahore where electricity never comes and bombs burst ten, ten times a day and the one thing, the *only* thing, I had was a maid and now even she's gone!"

"You'll find another maid."

"And who's going to train her? Teach her to knock before she comes in? And not call you 'bhaijan' and me 'baji' as if we were her older brother and sister? And get her to use a tooth-brush instead of a tree? And not to tell people I'm sitting on the toilet when they call? *You?*"

"Look," he said, switching on the TV and that also bore BBC news, "it's not the end of the world. You should just wish her well and start looking for someone else."

"She doesn't need my wishes. That snake-in-the-grass. She's going to be living it up with her white employers who say thank you thousand, thousand times and snatch our servants and spoil them forever with televisions and fridges. It's not fair!"

"It's hardly as if Jameela is going to Abu Dhabi to live it up in clubs and malls," sighed Janoo. "She's going to work as a domestic servant. And how do you know her white employers are going to shower her with goodies? From my experience, even bleeding-heart liberals revert pretty quick to colonial *sahibs* and *memsahibs* when they find themselves in places where help is cheap and has no rights. So if I were you I wouldn't begrudge her Abu Dhabi. Believe me you wouldn't want to change places with her."

"So then why did she—?"

He put the volume high up to shut me up. I *knew* I shouldn't have married him. At least he could have done some "look-at-her-what-a-back-stabber-may-she-rot-in-hell" talk with me. Like

Mummy did. Like Aunty Pussy did. But no. He has no feelings for me. Not even this much of sympathy. Even now after seventeen years of marriage, after everything I've done for him—working myself to the bones making sure nice, nice food is on the table, the generator is full of diesel, his computer, his TV, his everything is working first class, Kulchoo is having the best tuitions and our comings and goings are with the nice, rich, sophisty old-family-types of Lahore—and still, all he can think of is that snake Jameela's wellfear. One thing I know, I shouldn't have married him.

"You know something?" I said to his back. "You don't deserve me."

"Hmm?" he said, changing the channel.

"I said you don't deserve me."

"You can say *that* again!" he muttered to the TV screen.

"You should have married your Oxen *memsahib*. Both of you could have been good and holy together, always thinking of the wellfear of servants rather than your own families."

"Oh for God's sake! Is this tantrum because I expressed some sympathy for—"

"It's *not* a tantrum, okay? And just because I'm not an Oxen doesn't mean you can speak to me as if I was three years old. Tantrum, my shoe."

"If I'd known that this was what was awaiting me in Lahore, I wouldn't have bothered to drive three hours through horrendous traffic—"

"So who asked you to come? You should have stayed in your stinky, bore village. That's where you are happiest anyways.

Why bother coming here at all? It's hardly as if you come for my company. The second you come here you switch on the TV and that also to bore BBC. Do you ever ask me what I want to see? Or ask me about where-all I've gone, who-all I've met, what-all I've done? Never. Not for one second. And why? Because you don't give two hoops about me. That's why. You care more about the servants' wellfear than you do about your wife's. Admit it."

"God almighty! I really don't think I deserve this barrage of criticism—"

"No no, you can criticize me all day and all night and that's fine. I don't read newspapers, I don't do work, I don't know politics, I don't know econmics, I buy too much jewellery, I do kittys, I am total time-waste. But I can't say *one* word against you. If I'm such a time-waste why did you marry me then, *haan*?"

"It's a question I've often asked myself."

"You think I am happy with *you*? With your bore lectures and your stuppid village and the embarrassing fights you have with everyone everywhere. And over what? Iraq. Obama. Osama. America. Stuppid time-waste. As if you can change anything. A dead body is more fun than you."

"All I want is to watch a bit of TV and then have a bite and go to sleep. Is that too much to ask?"

"No. No. Nothing is too much for you. It's me who can't do this and can't do that. Can't go to coffee parties, can't find brides for Jonkers. But you're right. I shouldn't find brides for Jonkers. Because what do I know about happy marriages, *haan*?"

20 *October*

I'm so depress, so depress, that don't even ask. I have no maid
to take my clothes out of my wardrope and lay them out in
the morning. No maid to pick them off the floor at night and
take them away for washing. No maid to straighten my shoes
in lovely long lines in my dressing room. No maid to sort up
my underwears drawer. No maid to bring my tea in the morning.
To pull the curtains. To plumb up my cushions. To hand me
my bag as I leave the house. To take my bag as I re-enter the
house. To press my legs and massage my head. To get my
shawl when I feel cold. To switch on the AC when I feel hot.
To tell me who-all is doing what-all in Kulchoo's room upstairs
when his friends come. To always tell my mother-in-law I'm
out whenever she calls. To give me goss about Sunny, Mulloo,
and all that she's heard from their maids. Never to tell my
goss to anyone. Ever.

On top, I'm not speaking to Janoo. Because of our fight,
na. Hai, I'm so depress, so depress that don't even ask.

Sunny says *desi* maids are all back-stabbers like this only
and that I should get a Filipina. They cost as much as a middle
manager-type in a small business but they don't say please get
my husband a job, and my son admission in school and my

father out of jail and my mother into hospital. They just do their work and after two years they go. Done. You never even know how many brothers and sisters they have. Locals *tau* eat you alive with their demands, demands, demands. Unlike locals, Filipinas also know English and can help your children with their homework and because everyone knows how much they cost, they make you look rich. They also call you Madam which sounds more modern and classy than *Baji*.

I also used to have one. She was called Maria and she was from Vanilla, Filipines. She was always smiling but when the tsunami came in Vanilla she cried and wept and howled and said she had to go home, so being the soft-headed and gentle soul that I am, I gave her five hundred dollars and time off for two weeks and she never came back. I think so she got another job somewhere else. Very selfish they are, I must say. And then I found Jameela and so I thought *chalo*, never mind, if God takes with one hand He gives with the other. Even if He takes English-speaking smart Filipina and gives Punjabi-speaking illitred *desi*. One shouldn't complain because He is like that only.

Now Sunny is after me to get another Filipina but Mulloo says Natasha is *tau* still really anti them even three years after her Filipina left. She gave so much of trouble that don't even ask. Apparently she was having an affair with *both* the driver and the cook and also taking money from them both and when they found out about each other there was a huge *phudda* in her house with both of them rushing at each other with kitchen knives and car-jacks. Police had to come. So embarrassing.

No, no, I think so I'll wait for a *desi*. At least she will have the decency to have one affair at a time. First cook, then driver, then bearer, and then guard. Everyone has a turn and everyone is happy. Mummy is right, you know, all these people think about is You Know What.

21 October

Kulchoo's been home all day reading Facebook, because schools and colleges are all closed. Again. This time because the fundos have attacked Islamic University in Isloo and killed six students. Janoo's been muttering non-stop about Kulchoo's disrupted education. But I said (we've started speaking now but only little, little) he'll only get educated if he lives, no? Even though he's an Oxen, sometimes Janoo says such crack things.

Even when schools open danger won't go away. Because the fundos *tau* are here to stay, *na*. Where will they go? Kabul? Kashmir? Waziristan? And then they'll be back because they like it here with Sat TV and bazaars full of olive oils and imported cheeses. So I've told Kulchoo from now only that I won't let him out of my sights even. He'll go to school, with driver and armed guard, and come straight back and that's it. No roaming around, no friends' houses, no Pizza Hut, no DVD shops, no mini-golf, no nothing. Not even tuition. Of course he shouted and screamed and said I'm polaroid about the Talibans but I say better polaroid than dead. No?

I said to Janoo that we should leave Pakistan and go away somewhere for a while.

"Like where?" he said.

"Dubai," I said. I wanted to say London but servants in London are not nice, always wanting holidays on Sundays and so full of attitude, almost as if they didn't know they were servants. At least Dubai has good supply of Filipinas and South Indians who know they're servants. And they also speak nice English. Not like the illitreds here who can only speak Punjabi.

"And do what in Dubai?" asked Janoo.

"Live," I said.

All our friends have two, two passports. Sunny's father was born in London so she's got UK passport. Baby and Jamal have got Canadian. And they're all set with a three-bed apartment in Missy Saga in Toronto where all the *desis* live and now whenever anyone says things are going to the bogs in Pakistan they smile smugly and say nothing. And Aslam and Natasha have bought a house in Malaysia in Koala Lumpur because he's into rubber in a big way, so they're all right. Only Mulloo and Tony and we have nothing. Mulloo and Tony because they don't even have enough money left to bribe a lawyer or buy property over the seas but of course Mulloo won't admit and she says it's because she's a patriot and that she was born here and she'll die here. Janoo of course is just bore and says he's not going to dessert a sinking ship. I told him I'm not talking about the *Titanic*, you know. He said I might as well be. I think so he's lost it.

So then I said okay forget about me because obviously you don't give two hoops about whether I live or die but at least think of Kulchoo. And he said in three years Kulchoo would be going to university abroad and after that he could choose for himself whether he wanted to stay there or return home. And if things became too unsafe before then he would send Kulchoo to boarding school in England.

And I said what if things became too unsafe for me here? After all, bombs are bursting every day. People are dying, or being robbed by bugglers in their own houses and being shot and beaten also and only the other day I heard that someone who Nina knows had her arms slashed with a naked blade in Liberty Market by a beardo. He said he did it because she was wearing sleeveless.

"If you are worried about lawlessness in Lahore you can always come with me to Sharkpur," he said.

Sharkpur! His bore village, where all you can hear is the mooing of cows and the barking of his mother, the Old Bag, and the snorting of his sisters, the Gruesome Twosome. Where no one uses olive oil and everyone is so illitred that they haven't even heard of Prada or Versace. Where all you see is bore grass and even more bore fields and male sheeps misbehaving with female sheeps in front of everyone. And all you can do is sit there and pretend you haven't noticed the shameless sheep. Where there's no boutique, no spa, no hairdresser, no nice jeweller even. Honestly, I don't know how people survive there. No, not even my dead body would be happy there.

"Thanks, but no thanks," I said to Janoo. If I have to choose between dying of boredom or being blown up by a suicide bomber, I'll take the bomb. At least it's quicker.

Even bloody Jameela is living it up in Abu Dhabi while I die in bloody Lahore.

We had dinner at home. Just me and Janoo and Kulchoo. You know *na* that once the wedding and party season starts properly, we'll be out every single night for whole two months. Dinners, balls, musical evenings, parties, weddings, *milaads*, the whole deal. So it's good to have one night in. Also servants don't get too spoilt that way. Otherwise, every night the minute we leave, they sneak off back to their quarters. Lazy lumps.

Haan, so as soon as Kulchoo came home from his tuition master's at nine o'clock, I picked up the inner-com and told the bearer to bring the food on a trolley to my bedroom because my fave TV serial was on and in the dining room we have no TV. As yet.

Kulchoo flopped down on the sofa and sighed loudly.

I looked up from my TV serial and said, "Are you okay, baby?"

"Yeah," he said, making a face. I don't think so he likes me calling him baby. "I'm just tired."

"No tell, *na*, have you got headache? Tummy ache? Mosquito bites? Fever?" I pressed my hand on his forehead. It seemed hottish to me. I swear if anything happens to my baby I'm going to go and pull each and every one of Aunty Pussy's back-combed hairs from her head with my own hands.

"Chill, Mum," said Kulchoo pulling away. "I'm okay. I told you, I'm okay."

Janoo put down his papers and told me not to fuss. I ignored.

"Then what's the matter?" I asked. "Anyone said something to you? Tell me, and I'll go and see them and tell them what's what."

"Don't give me grief. I'm just tired. Okay? I've just had four hours of tuitions."

Poor thing, *na*, every day after school he goes to four different tuition masters' homes and has tuitions in four different subjects. Maths, Chemistry, Econmics, and Civics. Or is it Physics? My heart breaks but what to do? Everyone goes. Apparently it's the only way of getting As and place in a college with a good name in America. Places like Yales and Princedom and Havard. Janoo's always been against tuitions. He says it makes you dependent. And that Kulchoo's bright enough to do well on his own. All he needs to do is focus. As if our son was a microscope or something. But if we don't send Kulchoo everyone will say we are too mean to spend on our son even. And that we are throwing away his future.

"What I don't understand is why the tuition masters can't come to our house instead of you having to go to them?" I asked Kulchoo, giving sideways look to TV but it was where I'd left it; mother-in-law was still shouting at daughter-in-law for not bringing a house in her dowry. "Then you wouldn't have to get tired being driven here, there, and everywhere. You could just sit comfortably in your own sitting room and make them come here. After all, we pay them fifty thousand each. They can do this much for us. Baby was telling me the Maths tutor has got so rich so rich, he's got three flats in same building as theirs in Toronto. Three flats. *Ji haan*. One on top, two below. Three, three bedrooms each. Least he could do is to come here and—"

"Mum, we've been through this a hundred times. You *know* why I have to go there. Because they run classes for thirty boys at a time. Now please can we have dinner? I'm hungry. What's cooked?"

"What I don't understand is why you have to go to school at all?" said Janoo putting down his book with a thump on the sofa. "If you have to be taught all over again in a tuition centre by the very same people who are supposed to be teaching you at school, why bother going to school at all? For what?"

"I need my teachers' and my headmaster's recommendation to apply to uni, remember?"

"Ah, light dawns," said Janoo. "So the school fees are for the *recommendation*. And all along I thought I was paying for an *education*. Silly me!"

"Dad, don't be like that," said Kulchoo. "Besides I also have two Englishes and Pak Studies and Urdu and Islamiyat at school and for those I have no tuition."

"Don't eat the poor child's head," I said to Janoo. "Everyone does tuitions. Sunny's stuppid son does six. We don't want the whole world pointing fingers at us saying we're too mean to send our son to tuitions. And everyone also knows no teaching is done in school. If the masters taught in school who'd go to their tuition centres? And where would they make enough money to send their own kids to college in the US, *haan*? Have you seen the fees? You know how much it costs? So then? Why are you asking *faltoo* questions?"

"I don't see how this is a useless question. All I'm asking—"

Just then, thanks God, the food trolley came in. So I quickly heaped a plate with rice and chicken and *koftas* and put it in front of Kulchoo.

"Eat," I said.

"I'm not hungry," said Kulchoo.

"See what you've done?" I said to Janoo. "Taken away the child's hunger *and* made me miss my TV drama."

"It's you who started it," said Janoo. "Not just this conversation but the whole tuition nonsense. And all to keep up with the Joneses. I was against it right from the start."

"Joneses? Have you gone cracked? I don't know anyone called Joneses."

"For God's sake! It's just a figure of spee—"

"You know what, guys?" shouted Kulchoo. "I'm out of here." And he got up from the sofa and walked out slamming the door behind him.

"Kulchoo, eat something, baby," I called after him.

"I'll take something from the kitchen," came his faraway reply.

"Happy now?" I said to Janoo.

He opened his mouth to say something but then he shut it and quietly left the room. I looked at the TV but even the credits of my serial had finished. I sat there with the untouched trolley till the food got cold. But still no one came back. Then the bearer came and said that Saab had asked for a plate of food to be sent to his study. I told him to take the trolley away.

22 *October*

I'm *tau* very glad that the Talibans are being given a good and proper beating-up by the army. They were giving us no ends of trouble. Blowing themselves up in full bazaars at the least evocation. You want to blow yourself up, go do it inside your own home or out in some quiet corner where you don't endanger others, no? Honestly, so selfish they are. So unconsiderate. Then they were also stopping women in markets and bazaars and threating to throw acids in their faces if they wear jeans. Imagine! As if Pakistan belongs to them. And we are their slaves. Thanks God the army is showing them what's what. If you ask me, it was overdue. I hope so now they will finish them off once and for all and not do a little bit of killing and then go quietly behind our backsides and make up with them again and as a make-up present give them another chunk of the country. "Here take Swat. And, here's Kohat. Want Mardan also? *Chalo*, never mind, take that also."

I know there's that small problem of all the refugees who've fled from Waziristan to escape all that fighting-shighting and bombing-vombing. These days, by the ways, they are not called refugees but IDPs. That means Infernally Displaced Peoples. Sounds so much nicer than refugees, no? Almost as if it were a job title in a big company—like CFO, meaning Chief Federal Officer, or VP, meaning Vice President, although I always thought VP meant Visible Panties. Newspapers are saying there are a million IDPs in the refugee camps near Mardan. Really, the poors have so many children! Anyways, all the NGO-*wallahs* are making such a big hoo-haa that they are living in tents with no runny water and no toilets and no electricity and no schools and no doctors-shoctors and that something has to be done. I wanted to tell them that listen, I also live without electricity and no doctor-shoctor lives with me also but do I complain? But then I thought better not because then there will be another who-and-cry about how we rich don't understand anything.

Some of the mothers in Kulchoo's school have been sending the IDPs bus-fulls of bottled water and biscuits and dried milk and I asked what else they needed and they said that they needed clothes and medicine and the kids needed books. So being the soft-headed, charitable soul that I am, I packed up two enormous cardboard boxes for them and sent them along to Kulchoo's school. Honestly, nothing like doing charity to make you feel close to God.

Inside the boxes I put fourteen Mills and Boon novels and eighteen Barbara Cartland novels that I last read in June (including my favourite, *The Ruthless Rake*). I also put the last ten issues of *Good Times*, so the poor IDPs, they can also cheer up a little bit by looking at all the pictures of the best weddings and fab parties-sharties that we've been having here. Eight cartons of Lexxo (Lexotonil, my fave trankillizer) that I had left over. I think so they are slightly passed their expiry date, but I think so worst they will do is make the IDPs sleep longer. And if that refugee camp is as crowded as they say it is, it must be noisy also. So good to sleep longer, no? And then I sent them some old ties of Janoo's. Some *tau* were even designer like Armani and all but they were a bit old-fashioned type so I thought *chalo* some Pathan pheasant who's never worn Armani before will become so happy. I also sent some old chiffon saris of mine with matching petty-coats and blouses that are a bit on the tight side now.

Come to think of it, I don't think so I've seen Pathan women from the tribal areas wearing saris. Come to think of it, I don't think so I've ever seen a Pathan woman from the tribal areas. I don't think so anyone in the outside world has either. They're a bit like those rare animals in African forests that you can't see unless you go and live there in the heat and the damp with the mosquitoes and the snakes and no toilets for months and months, very quietly and never showing yourself and maybe, just maybe, one day you catch a glimpse of one. But *chalo*, poor things they can wear their chiffon saris underneath their *chaddars*. Like Saudi princesses who wear Versace minis under their *abayas*.

25 October

Last night was the Butt–Khan wedding. So all yesterday I was
on tender hooks. Because my sick-sense told me tonight at
this wedding, we'd find a girl for Jonkers. After all, every single
illegible girl of Lahore was going to be there—you don't show
up and everyone thinks you're the only poor loser who wasn't
invited to the wedding of the year. So even if you don't want
to, you go. For face.

At least three thousand people were invited. Because
between groom's father, Talwar Khan, and bride's father, Khayam
Butt, they knew everyone in the city. At least everyone who
was worth knowing and doing "hello–hi" with. So if a suitable
girl wasn't at *this* wedding then I don't know where she'd be.
And if Aunty Pussy couldn't find a candidate there, then I'm
sorry to say she might just have to design herself to her fate.

I wore my seven-standed emerald, pearl and diamond necklace that had belonged to Janoo's grandmother with the matching
earrings. Because I knew there'd be lots of BNM—Big New
Money—there. That's why I chose my "we-were-here-first"
hairloom jewellery. After all you've got to show people that even
though you may not arrive in a sport car, it doesn't mean you
are hungry-naked.

Of course, kill-joy Janoo didn't come. He said it would be mega circus, heaving with boot-lickers and arse-holes, and that no one would notice if he didn't show up. I told him that even if ten thousand people were invited, our hosts would know immediately that he hadn't come, not because he's special but because they keep taps on who-all came and who-all didn't and they would remember and they would mind and tomorrow Kulchoo would be growing up and with grace of Allah be getting married and if Janoo didn't bother to go to anyone's weddings today nobody would come to Kulchoo's wedding tomorrow and everybody would say, "*Haw*, poor things, what a disaster their wedding was." And he said that he didn't care and I said fine, be like that and I was going and he said be my guest. I said, no *ji*, I'd be Khayam Butt and Talwar Khan's guest. It's not *your* wedding, okay? And then he said something back and then I said something back and then it became a proper fight with him shouting at me for being shallow and stupid and me shouting at him for being bore and a loser and now he's gone off in a puff to Sharkpur. Good radiance!

So where was I? *Haan*, at the wedding. It was at the Royal Elephant Club, *na*. After the Marriott bomb wedding-sheddings are not in hotels any more. Too much of security headache because anyone can walk into a hotel and blow themselves up. Not like reclusive clubs where only members can blow themselves up. The reception was in a big tent on the front lawns. It wasn't cold enough to need a tent but I think so they got it because of security. At the entrance they had those empty doorway-type things like they do at airports that you have to step through. Thanks God the people doing the checking didn't prod and poke us and go through our handbags and open our lipsticks and say "*Hai,* what nice shade, is it from foreign?" like those greedy police-type women do at the airport. Anyways, they should know it's not the well-offs like us, but the hungry-nakeds who do the suicide bombings.

The wedding tent was fab. Customs-made of course—all red velvet, red lanterns, and golden satin bows. I think so the theme was Chinese New Years or was it Moulin Rogue? Whatever it was, it was to die for. Everywhere there were big red lilies—hung from the ceiling and in huge golden vases, standing on golden stands. Mulloo had already said they'd come from Holland, the lilies, not the stands, and that they'd costed forty *lakhs.* The tent was bulging with people. So thanks God there was air conditioning.

Everyone was there—my coffee group, my kitty group, my charity group, relatives, relatives of relatives, old school friends, new society friends—honestly, it's so nice to be so well reknowned. At once I started mingling-shingling, chatting away, while also scanning the crowds for a pretty girl. One thing I'll say about me: unlike that bitch Jameela, I'm the loyal type. I never start enjoying myself so much that I forget why I'm there.

And then I spotted Shabnam Butt, the bride's mother, shadowed by a servant girl. At once I made a bee-hive for her. You have to register your attendance, *na,* otherwise who's to know whether you came or not? I had in my hand a pink silk purse—paper envelopes are *tau* so past it—on top of which I'd had "congratulations" embroidered in thick, gold thread. Inside it

I'd put a tiny name card and five thou in crisp new notes. Wedding present, *na*. We give five at weddings of distants— for nears and dears we give ten. And for family we give fifty— unless it's Janoo's family, when I give less. But while I was putting the money into the silk purse I thought that these people probably give five as tips to their servants, being so rich and all.

I tapped Shabnam on her shoulder. Slowly she turned around. Hanging around her neck was a bib coming down to her waste, like babies wear, but made of diamonds. Promise by God. Matching diamond purses on diamond chains hung from her ears. Her mud-brown face was caked with white foundation. She looked at me through half-closed eyes ringed by fake lashes that were like thorn hedges.

"Hello, *jaan*," she murmured.

"Congratulations," I said, pressing the purse into her hands. "What a fab necklace."

"Thanks, yours is sweet too." Holding my gift by a finger and thumb, like it was a used tissue, she passed it to her maid. The maid rubbed it between her fingers and thumb. I think so she was checking how many notes I'd given. I knew it! I should have given ten. I looked away as she dropped the purse into a fat, zipped General Life Insurance bag she'd got cramped in her armpit.

"How nicely you've done all this," I said to Shabnam, waving a hand around at the tent and flowers and all.

"Event managers," she murmured. "Why to take tension? What's money for, if you have to take tension? Hmm?"

Then she just turned and went. Without a bye-bye, or have a nice time, or thank you for coming even.

Where was Mummy? And Aunty Pussy? After all, I was here for them only. And that stuppid Jonkers. Last thing I wanted was to come to this circus and be pushed around by noovo-rich loser-types in their over jewellery who couldn't recognize hairlooms when they saw them. Sweet, she called my necklace, as if it was some two-*paisa* plastic locket from Anarkali. What cheeks!

Suddenly, I saw Mulloo waving from the distance. Thanks God for friends. She was with her daughter, Irum. Irum is seventeen. Between you, me and the four walls, she's a bit young to be paraded around at weddings in the hope of attracting proposals. But as Janoo says to Kulchoo, who is always late for school, early bird gets the worm. And because of Tony's factory closing and him defaulting on all those loans he'd taken from guvmunt banks I think so they need to marry Irum off richly. And quickly.

Mulloo was wearing a sequenced sari I'd seen twenty times before and so much of blush that she looked as if she'd just been given two tight slaps. A thin little choker with tiny, tiny diamonds was buried in roles of fat in her throat. She grinned at me. I wondered if I should tell her that she had lipstick on her teeth. She noted my necklace with her slitty little eyes but didn't compliment. Typical.

"Mulloo, sweetie, you have lipstick on your teeth."

"Ammi," Irum said to Mulloo, "I'm going to hang with my friends. You've got Aunty here with you now. Byee." And she went off in a swish of pink chiffon the exact same colour of Rose Petal toilet tissue.

"Has your husband come?" Mulloo asked me. "Or has he abandoned you for his village again? Better watch out, sweetie, you know feudals can get up to all sorts of naughty things." She laughed fakely.

"Janoo's got flu. Where's Tony?"

"Inside only. Khayam's arranged a big bar there in one of the upstairs rooms. I've heard he's spent seven million on booze alone. Seven! Sunny was saying that last week when Akbar called his bootlegger for his usual whisky–vodka order, he said: 'Sorry Saab, Khayam Saab's cleaned out all of Lahore and half of Islamabad also. You'll have to wait after New Year's now. Then I'll get some for you from the embassies in Islamabad.' He has a special relationship with the Russian ambassador's cook, *na*."

"And this tent and stands and lanterns they've had made specially and everything, that must have cost Shabnam and Khayam also," I said.

"Two arms, two legs, and I don't know what else. But as I always say," she said lowering her voice and leaning into me, "who are they trying to impress, hmm? I have seen it all before. A hundred, hundred times."

"And frankly," I whispered back, "between you, me, and the four walls, that necklace that Shabnam is wearing—so gody, so new-new and recent-looking. But then what can you expect from someone whose name even no one had heard nine years ago?"

"Eight," said Mulloo. "That's when they got that first contract on that Gulberg children's park, don't you remember? When he persuaded," she rubbed thumb and fingers together, "Talwar Khan to fence off the public park and turn it into townhouses?"

"I know," I said. "Before that *tau* they were total non-identities."

Just then my mobile rang. It was Mummy.

"*Where are you?*" she shrieked. "Me and Pussy and Jonkers, we've been sitting here at this bloody wedding for nearly *two hours*. Our bottoms have gone to sleep."

"How many times have I told you, Mummy, to come on time?" I shouted back. Honestly, these old-types, they have no sense of time. They think just because card says nine it means nine. Hundred, hundred times I've told Mummy nine means eleven. Hopefully that stuppid Jonkers hadn't shown up wearing a safari suit and looking like a low-level bureau-cat. "Honestly, why don't you ever *listen*? Where are you sitting? Okay, okay, stay there. I'm coming." I shut up the phone.

"Your aunty still looking for girl?" Mulloo asked, checking her lipstick in her compact mirror.

I was not befooled by her casual enquiry. Not for one second even. She's always up to some little plot or plan or something. One thing about Mulloo, she's very sly. Can't let your guards down with her.

"Girls, *tau,* as you know, are plenty," I said casually. "But we are picky, you know. Not like all these easily satisfied people who'll be happy with first thing they see."

"Of course, darling, of course," she smiled, closing her compact with a tight little click, as if that was final word on everything. "Shall we go find your mother?" She linked her arm in mine and because I didn't know how to shake her off I had to take her along—like chewing gum under my shoe.

Because Mummy and Aunty Pussy are so early for everything they always manage to grab the best seats. Now they were right by the stage where bride and groom were sitting, on the seats that are normally reserved for the in-laws. You know, *na*, that once Mummy decides she's going to sit somewhere not even wild asses can move her. So there they were, sitting in the best seats. Everyone who went to congratulate the bridal couple and press envelopes into their hands had to pass by them. Best place for checking out prospectus girls.

Mummy's always said that Aunty Pussy is at least three years older than her and that she lies about her age because she failed one year in school and had to repeat again, but tonight they were both looking like twins, with their maroon hair teased and sprayed into big stiff bubbles on top of their heads and eyeshadow in the creases of their eyelids and long diamond earrings dragging down their wrinkled ear lopes.

Jonkers was standing behind them gripping the backs of their chairs. He was wearing suit and tie and looking as if he was going in for root canal. His forehead was shiny with sweat.

"Hello, Aunties, so nice you look," Mulloo gushed.

"Hello, darling," Mummy said to me. "Lovely jewellery. Doesn't she look like a princess, Pussy? What a surprise to see *you* here, Mulloo."

"Hi, Jonkers," I said, patting his shoulder. It felt stiff as cardboard. "Relax *yaar*," I whispered to him.

"Hello, Apa," he mumbled.

"At last!" Aunty Pussy said to me. "I thought you were never going to show up. What's the time? Have you found any girls?"

"Oho, Aunty," I said. "At least give us time to sit down."

The bride and groom were sitting on golden thrones on the stage and their mothers and fathers and brothers and sisters were all sitting on red sofas besides them. They were posing for pictures, with their teeth showing in fake grins. Video-*wallahs* and camera men hoovered around like flies in front of them shouting instructions, "This way please. Please to look straight." And guests waited below the stage to go and hand their envelopes.

"Who's that girl?" Aunty Pussy spotted a girl standing near the bottom of the stage and waved her hand up and down at her like she was calling a taxi. Mummy slapped her hand down.

"Pussy! Behave."

"Which one, Aunty?" asked Mulloo.

"*That* one. The one in the mauve and pink. Nice, big emeralds. Looks to be from a good home. No, Jonkers?"

Before Jonkers could open his mouth, Mulloo leapt in.

"You mean the busty one with the backless blouse and the big bottom? That one? Turn your eyes away right now, Aunty. Bite your tongue. Don't even take her name. You know what she's called? Speedboat! I don't think you need me to tell you why." And then she told us why. "She was four years up from my Irum at school and from age twelve she was *khisskoing*, you know sneaking off, from school with strange men. Not boys, Aunty. Men. *Men*. Otherwise she comes from good enough home. Father is Magic Carpets and mother is harmless. Does charity."

"Oh no, no, no," says Aunty Pussy. "*Last* thing we need is another fast number for my poor, innocent Jonkers. What about that one then, the tall, fair one at the back? In blue."

"I don't think—" started Jonkers but Mulloo cut in.

"Naila? Oh, she's engaged, Aunty. Big shame you missed her. Got engaged just last month. *Such* a nice girl. So polite, so well-brought-up. She is Ahmed and Nikky Shah's daughter. Nice, decent people with nice, decent house in Islamabad and nice, decent lands near Faisalabad."

"Why did we miss her? Why didn't you suggest her before?" Aunty Pussy glared at me.

"*Uff Allah*, Aunty," I sighed. "She's got engaged to her father's younger brother's son. I think so they must have had an understanding in the family from before only. Probably from when they were children. You know how these landed types are. Like to keep the lands in the family."

"Well *your* husband's landed, isn't he? And he married *you*," Aunty Pussy said to me. The way she said, *you*, as if Janoo had married some cockroach.

"Yes, but Janoo's not any old feudal. He's an Oxen, and in case you don't know, Aunty Pussy," I told her, "that's someone who's studied from Oxford."

After that, I decided I'm not going to point out a single girl to Aunty Pussy. I damn care if Jonkers dies a poor left-over bachelor. In any case, there's bossy-body Mulloo to look after him.

"All these new people everywhere," Mummy murmured. "We never saw them before, did we, Pussy? Where have they come from? But look there. The girl behind that fat man. I know her family, Pussy."

"Which one?" Aunty Pussy leaned so far ahead in her chair that Jonkers had to grab the back of it to stop her falling face forward into the carpet.

"There, see? The one who's laughing? She's Sultana Subhan's granddaughter. You remember Sultana, don't you, Pussy? She was with me in class, long plait, down to her knees. Three years junior to you. Married very young. Wealthy family, Pussy, and old, from Karachi."

"*One* year junior," said Aunty Pussy sourly.

"Nice girl," agreed Mulloo, "but no point, really. She's becoming an architect or a doctor or something at some college in America and you know how bossy over-educated girls can be and anyway by the time she finishes her studies—"

"My Jonkers can't wait," declared Aunty Pussy. "He's waited long enough. Isn't that so, darling?" she said, suddenly remembering her silent son. "He must be married by the end of the year. Latest."

Jonkers made some gargling-type noise in his throat but Aunty Pussy ignored.

Aunty Pussy saw two more girls. Mulloo immediately told her they were married. One had a child even. Aunty Pussy kept asking about more and more girls, and Mulloo kept rejecting them, saying this is wrong with this one and that is wrong with that. I think so Mulloo was doing all the rejecting because she was plotting some plot of her own. She's like that. Plotty.

I looked at my watch. It was quarter to midnight. When would they serve dinner? Not that it would be any great feast. Not since the spoil-sport guvmunt announced that weddings must have one dish only. Now instead of the fifteen-dish dinners we used to have there's only bore *qorma*. But if the guvmunt's trying to stop people spending so much on weddings I think so it should see Khayam's booze bill and Shabnam's diamonds, not to mention the Holland lilies. I was so hungry, I'd even settle for bore *qorma*.

Aunty Pussy saw an old friend and struggled up from her chair to go and do hello–hi, but her foot caught in the carpet and she went flying. But thanks God a girl was passing in front of her just then and she managed to catch Aunty Pussy before she crashed to the ground.

"Are you all right?" she asked, holding Aunty Pussy by the shoulders.

"Yes, yes, fine," Aunty Pussy snapped, brushing the girl's hands off her shoulders as if they were dandrough. "I'm perfectly fine. Can't you see?"

I wish Aunty Pussy wouldn't treat everyone like a servant. Honestly, some times she can be so rude.

"Thank you," said Jonkers to the girl. He stepped up and helped Aunty Pussy back into her chair. "Thank you for saving my mother." He was probably also feeling embarrassed of his mother's behaviour.

"No problem." The girl smiled at him.

Jonkers' face flashed red.

She had a dimply smile, otherwise she was a bit plainish. High pony tail, slim, wheatish colouring, longish nose. She was dressed in a pale yellow silk *shalwar kameez* with just a little bit of silver embroidery on the neckline and small pearl earrings. No designer shoes, no big jewels, no nothing. She didn't look like she came from an effluent bagground. Aunty Pussy thought the same because she gave her one look and immediately lost interest. The girl gave Jonkers a little wave and went away.

"What did you think?" asked Jonkers, tugging at my elbow.

"Of what?" I asked.

"That girl. The one in yellow? Who just passed by?"

"That dark, poor-looking thing in the cheap clothes?" asked Aunty Pussy in a loud voice. "She must be one of the poor relations. Or else, a gatecrasher."

Immediately Jonkers' face fell down but he didn't say anything.

And then I saw Sunny and Faiza standing gossiping and they called me over and I went because Mulloo was jumping up and down on my nerves. I did just five minutes of goss with them and when I came back I saw that Jonkers was gone and Aunty Pussy and Mulloo were smiling as if they'd just got engaged to each other.

"It's been decided," said Aunty Pussy when she saw me. "Your lovely friend here, what's your name, dear? Yes of course, Mottoo. Well Mottoo—"

"Mulloo, Aunty, my name is Mulloo, not Mottoo."

"Yes, yes, Mottoo has a cousin with a lovely daughter. Young, respectful, wealthy, nicely brought-up, isn't that right? Who she's going to introduce to us."

"Why?" I asked, giving Mulloo a suspicious look.

"For your cousin Jonkers, of course."

Bloody Mulloo. She's so pushy. Always pushing herself to the front. Well, I damn care what sort of girl she gets for Jonkers now. Aunty Pussy and she deserve one another. And if Jonkers is going to be such a wet brag and just stand there gargling and staring, then he also deserves whatever type of cheapster thing or bore number they give him.

"Jonky darling, have you heard? You're marrying Mottoo's cousin. Jonky?" Aunty Pussy's head snivelled around to look at the empty space where he'd been standing. "Where is he? Where's he gone?"

"I'll go find him, Aunty." Mulloo, grinning like a baboon, went off to look for him.

"He's probably gone to find some dinner," said Mummy. "Get up, Pussy. We'd better go and get something to eat also before we all starve to death." And when they'd gone a bit of the way, I heard her say to Aunty Pussy, "You shouldn't say that you're going to marry Mulloo's cousin's daughter. You haven't even seen her yet. She may be a hunchback or black as coal, for all you know."

27 *October*

This morning I was woken up at the crack of noon by a phone call. Who else but Aunty Pussy? Honestly, she's so consistent, so consistent that don't even ask. Once she's got after something only a suicide bomber could make her change her mind.

"Dar-*ling*," she shrieked, "your Mummy seems to think that you got upset at the wedding. Why, darling? What is that Mottoo to me? It is *you* who will choose Jonky's future brides with me. She can show me all she wants, but *you're* the one who's going to have final say. After all, you are blood."

And then she told me about Mulloo's distant cousin.

Apparently she has a broken *nikah* behind her so, like Jonkers, she is also second-hand. And she is quiet and simple and obedient. And rich. Her father has a big import–export business and they have a nice, fat house in Defence Housing Society but not near the bad bit of Defence where all the prostitutes are. Mulloo (trust her, the pushy back-stabber), she's already organized a tea party at their house for Aunty Pussy. I told Aunty Pussy to take Jonkers along as well so the girl and boy could see each other but she fell silent for a bit and then said Mulloo had told her that maybe not at the first meeting, because her cousin, Farva, is in that way a little bit on the conservative side. Not much. A bit, only.

They must be *pukka* conservative-types to do *nikah* contract instead of just engagement. Breaking it off is like doing proper die-vorce through courts and all, unlike engagement that you can break any time, anywhere. I bet you Mulloo's cousin did the *nikah* when her daughter was a baby or something. Poor Jonkers. He's marrying into a fundo family.

Aunty Pussy begged me to come along also. I wanted to say no, you go with your precious Mulloo, but then thinking of Kulchoo I said yes. Before I hanged up, I asked Aunty Pussy if she'd told Zeenat Kuraishi that Jonkers wasn't interested. And Aunty Pussy at once became sharp with me and said how could she go and say they were not interested when Zeenat hadn't even asked properly. When the right moment came, she'd drop a hint. Until then she was going to let sleeping logs lie. So after that I called Mummy and told her that she must come also because Aunty Pussy when she gets highly stung like this, she can become quite over, *na*. Mummy said okay.

After that I called Jonkers in his towel and bed-sheet office and told him we were going to see Girl Number Two the next day. I also told him that he couldn't come just now because her parents were a little bit like that. I thought he'd be really disappointed but he seemed least bothered as if he couldn't care less if he came or not. I said to him sharply, I said, "I'm doing this for you, okay?" So he thanked me and said he was very grateful to me for taking time out like this. I asked if he had any last requests. Nothing really, he said, except that girl must be nice person and must be someone who would be on his side. That's two things, I told him. And anyways, what did he mean by "on his side"? Supportive, he said. I told him we were going to look at a girl, not a sports bra, okay?

28 *October*

Mulloo's cousin lives in a powder-palace. It has two storeys and is plastered everywhere in white plaster—white pillars, white dome, white triangle, paper-hat-type thing on front porch. All powder-pashas—drugs smugglers, *na*—have houses like this. I think so they must be having a textbook of house designs for drug smugglers from which they all copy. Also house is in Defence Phase V, on the very edge of Lahore, where all the upstarters live. The army only started making it into plots and selling to people five years ago. Before that it was boarder with India.

"What did Mulloo say her cousin's husband did?" asked Mummy, as the driver honked at the gate.

"All Mulloo's told me is that girl is called Tasbeeh, she is in her early twenties and that the family is well off," Aunty Pussy told her. "And she's got a broken *nikah*."

"Didn't someone say he did import–export?" I asked.

"This looks more like the house," said Mummy, "of someone who only *exports*, Pussy, if you get my meaning."

"It's not nice to judge people like that," said Aunty Pussy with a holy look, "before you've even done hello–hi with them."

I wondered inside my heart whether Aunty Pussy would be as holy if the house had been small and poor-looking.

A tiny window in the big iron gate opened and someone from inside checked us out. Then seeing it was us, rich-type ladies from good baggrounds in nice salon car, the armed guards—nine of them, I counted—opened the gate and we drove in. The house was big and it had taken over most of the plot, leaving only stripes of lawn on the sides, like thin sideburns on a very fat face. There were no trees in the garden but lots of lamp-posts and a plaster statue of a girl in a bonnet and skirt. I think so she was Little Bore Peep or maybe Little Miss Muff It. Also parked in the drive were three big Land Cruiser jeeps with black windows. Mummy looked at the cars and gave me a look.

Mulloo was supposed to meet us here but at last minute she called and cancelled. She said her tummy was feeling upset. But that her cousin was expecting us.

The front door was opened by a barefoot servant man who needed a shave. He took us into the sitting room. It was a big room with big golden sofas spread with white crochay mats where you're supposed to rest your head and hands. There were no paintings on the walls, only a big print of a verse from the Holy Koran in a golden frame. There were no flowers and no decoration pieces on the tables, accept for a family of smiling Sarvoski hedgehogs. Mother with four babies.

Mulloo's cousin was shortish and plumpish and dressed in a long-sleeved, high-necked *shalwar kameez*. Around her neck from a gold chain, not a chain, more a rope, hung a big Allah pendant with big diamonds entrusted in it. Her head was covered in a polyester *hijab* that sat low on her forehead.

"*Assalam aleikum,*" she said, raising her hand to her forehead. "I'm Farva, Mulloo's cousin-sister, and I am sorry I was
not standing at the door to greet you but I was saying my
prayers." She gave a happy little laugh. "My prayers are a little
longer than other people's because I have so much to thank
Almighty Allah for. Even if I lie with my forehead to the ground
all day, all night before Him, it would not be enough. So much
He has blessed me. Will you take something cold?"

Before we could tell her she called loudly for the servant.

"Siraj! Siraj! *Siraj!*" When he didn't come she stamped off
into the kitchen and from there we heard her shouting. "Where
do you all disappear to? What do I pay you for? Why haven't
you given drinks?" Then she came back into the room followed
by the unshaven Siraj and also another manservant with greasy
hair and asked with another happy laugh, "Coke? Sprite? Fanta?"

We said no but she said no, no we must have something
and told Siraj to get three Cokes.

"You must be Mulloo's friend," she said turning to me. Her
eyes wandered disprovingly over my naked arms. "So much she
has told me about you. And you must be boy's Mummy?" she
asked Aunty Pussy.

"Yes, I am Parisa. My son—"

"Oh yes, yes, Mulloo told me. Jehangir his name is, no?
Has degree from foreign college. Has English pet name.
Conkers? Bonkers?"

"Jonkers," said Aunty Pussy coldly.

"Oh yes, sorry, sorry," Farva slapped her forehead. "What to
do? My memory is going away."

"I don't know if Mulloo has told you," began Aunty Pussy. She stopped because Siraj had come back with the Coke. He gave us a glass each with a soggy tissue half stuck to the underneath. Aunty Pussy quickly dropped the tissue into an ashtray. She put the glass down and began again, "I don't know if Mulloo has told you, but my son was married before. It is best to be frank from the start so there is no misunderstanding later. Marriage didn't last long and, Allah was merciful, there were no children."

Farva nodded. "Why did marriage break?"

"She was not, er, suitable."

"How?"

Aunty Pussy looked at me.

"She wasn't from our bagground," I said. "Didn't fit us."

"And because she didn't fit," added Mummy, "we thought, why waste time? So we quickly did die-vorce. Best is not to drag these things along."

"You *can* do die-vorce," said Farva, nodding hard. "It is in Islam. You are allowed. Please don't worry. I am very understanding that way. Tasbeeh, my elder daughter, also had a *nikah* you know. But we had to break it. Even though he was Tasbeeh's cousin-brother—her father's own brother's son. Because we discovered that he was not nice, even though he had grown up in front of our own eyes. He drank. Yes, I know you will not believe it, but he drank. Kept bad company, men who kept drink in their houses. As soon as I found out, I told Tasbeeh's father, 'I know he is your brother's son but I cannot have a son-in-law who drinks. My daughters have had a strict, religious

bringing up. I am not going to give them to men who drink.'
So next day, we broke it. It wasn't easy you know. Because we
had to go to courts and all, but we did it. Without telling
Tasbeeh even, we just went and broke it. And Tasbeeh accepted
because she knows what we do is always best. She is a good
girl, my Tasbeeh."

"What does Tasbeeh's father do, if you don't mind telling?"
asked Mummy

"By the grace of Almighty Allah, he has import–export
business."

"And what does he import and what does he export?"

"You will not believe but I have never even asked. So little
interest I take in worldly matters. What Allah gives, He gives.
Why to question? You are not drinking your Coke. Why they
are taking so long with tea? Servants! So lazy, no?"

And again she shouted for Siraj. When he came, she barked
at him to bring tea.

"With everything, okay?"

"Er, can we, um," I asked quietly, because you never know
with these *hijabi* types, "meet Tasbeeh? Is she inside?"

"Surely, surely. I am very modern that way. I will go and
fetch her." She went off, her bottom bouncing like a basket-
ball behind her.

Mummy, me, and Aunty Pussy, we all looked at each other.

"You know, Pussy, don't you, that the Coke was flat?" Mummy
said in a low voice. "And those tissues!"

"Don't be such a snob, Malika."

"And we still don't know what the father does," I whispered.

"Why must you be so suspicious?" Aunty Pussy snapped at me softly. "After all, Jonkers also does export. Are you meaning that Jonkers is also doing hanky-panky?"

"He exports *towels*, Aunty. There's a difference between towels and—"

"And what?"

"You *know* what!" said Mummy.

"*And* she wears *hijab and* the furniture is so tacky *and*—"

"Here she is." Farva came back. Behind her was an even shorter but thanks God not plumper person than herself. "Tasbeeh, daughter, do *salaam* to aunties."

"*Assalam aleikum,*" mumbled Tasbeeh staring at the floor. She was also wearing high-necked *shalwar kameez*. It was brown with big, big orange flowers. She was not in *hijab*, thanks God, but her head was covered in a brown *dupatta*. She wore her long hair in a plait like that traitor, Jameela, used to. Her only make-up was some black under the eyes and very wrong orange lipstick.

"Do special salaams to *that* aunty." Farva pushed her at Aunty Pussy.

With bowed head, Tasbeeh went to Aunty Pussy's armchair and said *salaam* again.

Aunty Pussy got up and patted Tasbeeh on the head. Even though Aunty Pussy is not, you know, specially tall, Tasbeeh hardly went up to her shoulder. Aunty Pussy gave her three more pats, but she still stood there, eyes downcasted. So Aunty Pussy also stood there stiffly like a rooster, until I patted the sofa besides me.

"Come sit with me, Tasbeeh."

Tasbeeh looked at her mother and only when she nodded, she came over and sat besides me. She moved her bottom backwards on the sofa until her brown rubber-souled sandals were hanging three inches off the floor. Aunty Pussy sank thankfully back into her chair.

A strong smell of fried meat came into the room.

"Oh, good. Tea is coming," beamed Farva. "I hope you like kebabs. Tasbeeh's father always says my kebabs are best."

"Are you at college?" I asked Tasbeeh.

"No, I—" she began.

"She's finished," said Farva from across the room. "Did it in Islamiyat and Geography. BA. Good marks she got. By grace of Almighty Allah."

"When did you graduate?" I asked.

"Full one year and four months it will be at end of this month," replied Farva. "No, Tasbeeh, daughter?"

Tasbeeh nodded.

"So you've been at home since then?" I lowered my voice so that Farva couldn't hear and answer again.

"Mostly," whispered Tasbeeh, looking at her lap.

But Farva had the ears of a labradog. I swear she could probably make them stand up if she wanted.

"No you've been to Makkah *shareef* with us to do Umra and after that we took both you sisters to Dubai to buy your dowries," said Farva. "All those diamond sets we bought you, you've forgotten, hmm?"

Tasbeeh's reply was drowned out by a loud rattling and

creaking as if an old gate was being forced open and Siraj
and the other servant arrived pushing a wooden tea trolley
with big golden wheels. The tea cosy was in the shape of a
smiling blonde girl wearing a big bouncy skirt and a wide hat.
The downstairs bit of the tea trolley was loaded with fried
food—*pakoras*, *samosas*, kebabs, *jalebis*, and a huge bottle of
tomato ketchup. There was also a cake. Farva put a hand up
the blonde's skirt and pulled out a teapot and without asking
if we took milk or not poured out three cups with lots of milk
and told Tasbeeh to give to us. Then Siraj pushed the fried
food under our noses. When I saw those long oily roles of
meat, my *tau* stomach almost came rushing up my throat so
I said that no thank you, but I'm a vegetarian. So then Farva
insisted I have the potato *samosas* but I told her that I can't
take either *samosas*, or *pakoras*, or *jalebis* because of my choles-
troils.

Farva frowned and then she looked at Mummy and Aunty
Pussy who had also said no. "I know what you are doing. You
are being formal. Please take, otherwise I will mind. Tasbeeh,
daughter, give to Aunties." Then she said if we didn't have
cake, she wouldn't talk to us.

So I had a tiny slither. It was dry inside.

We sat for another half-hour drinking her milky tea and
hearing all about how many sheeps they slaughtered at the
last Eid—and that also on their driveaway, imagine!—and
how her husband liked doing it himself with his own hands
because it was duty of every good Muslim man to do it himself
with his own hands and how much meat they had given to

their neighbours and how much they had frozen themselves and that these kebabs she was giving us now were made out of those very same frozen minced sheeps.

In all of this she never for one second asked anything about Jonkers or us because I think so she must have taken all details about bagground—bank account, real state, age, job, degrees, looks, previous marriage, everything—from Mulloo before only. And nor did she let Tasbeeh say one word.

In the middle, the electricity went away and Farva shouted at Siraj to switch on the generator. Throughout she kept talking and laughing happily and Tasbeeh sat still and silent as if she'd slipped into a comma. I'd given up by now trying to get Tasbeeh to talk and so I also just stirred my tea and stared at the big circles of grease going round and round on top. Aunty Pussy looked fakely interested in Farva's conversation but Mummy's face was like a shop whose metal shutters had been pulled down and locked up and the shopkeeper had gone home for the night.

At last when Farva put her tongue inside her mouth for five minutes, Mummy and I jumped up and said thank you and that we must go home now. Please.

"So quickly?" said Farva.

"No, it hasn't been quick at all," said Mummy heavily, frowning at Aunty Pussy who was still sitting in her chair.

When she was seeing us all to the door Farva held my hand and said, "You know I've already started thinking of you like a big sister. So much I'm looking forward to seeing you again and again."

What cheeks! Big sister, my shoe! She must be at least ten years older than me. I smiled stiffly and took my hand back. No way was she becoming my relative. Money or no money.

Night had fallen down by the time we left. All the lamps had come on in Farva's empty garden. Outlined against the dark sky, her glittering white house looked like it was made of salt.

On the way home we were quiet for a bit and then in a fakely cheerful voice, Aunty Pussy said, "That wasn't too bad, was it? Of course they aren't classy like the Kuraishis and not so educated also, but girl seems a sweet, respectful type. The mother's a bit—"

"For God's sake, Pussy!" Mummy burst out. "They are not right and you know it."

"Why? What's wrong with them?" Aunty Pussy lifted her thin, pencilled eyebrows at us.

"*Wrong?*" shrieked Mummy. "What's right? The father is a drug smuggler. No there's no point denying, Pussy, I can tell from just looking at the house. Tell me, who has nine guards in his house? *Nine!* And why the black-out windows and those searchlights? And he slaughters sheep on his front drive with his own hands and the servants are unshaven and I'm sorry but they have no class. At all!"

"And I suppose you are perfect!" snapped Aunty Pussy. "From everywhere."

"Why did you take me if you don't want to hear what I have to say?" snapped Mummy back. "You've just sniffed money, Pussy, that's all. Be frank."

"You want my Jonkers to marry a *fakir*? Is that what you want? You're jealous. Be frank yourself."

"*Please!*" I cried. "Honestly, look at you! Such fighter cocks you two've become. Mummy shouldn't have said like that, Aunty Pussy, but what she says is right. They are not right. I don't know about the drugs-shrugs but they are not from our bagground, that much I could tell from their drawing room only. And if poor old Jonkers, at the age of thirty-seven, has to go and hide like a schoolboy every time he wants to drink a drink, what's the point of getting married and having your own set-up and everything? And anyways, I don't think so the girl will suit him. She *tau* poor thing is not even on her own side, let alone being on anyone else's side."

Aunty Pussy didn't say anything after that. She turned her face away and stared out of the window. I think so she was skulking. And Mummy in her corner was also skulking. Her mouth was a tight, little line. Thanks God I was sitting in front with the driver and didn't have to sit in between and take all the tension they were giving off. Inside my heart I thought, *haw*, look at Mulloo. I knew she wouldn't hand us a pretty, rich rellie, that much I was ready for, but I wasn't expecting a powder-pasha's dwarf daughter who has a fundo for a mother. Honestly. And she calls herself my friend. I bet she must be getting some bribe from Farva for finding her a nice, decent son-in-law from oldish family. Well, I'll also see how Farva becomes Jonkers' mother-in-law and Mulloo gets her bribe!

Because it was evening time when most people come out, there was a big traffic jam on Cavalry Grounds main road.

Cars, motorbikes, minibuses, donkey carts, rickshaws, bikes were all mixed up on the thin road leading to Gulberg Bridge. We were standing still but everyone was running their engines—accept the bikes and the donkeys—and the air smelt of petrol and dust and chicken *tikkas* from roadside stalls, so I put up my window and switched on the AC. I thought to myself what if someone was to burst a suicide bomb now. What would become of us? We would all become *tikkas*, that's what. For a moment I wanted to open the door and run out and run and run and never come back. But then I took a big breath and told myself everything was okay.

29 October

What a fab bash my friend Sara threw for her jewellery. She lives in Hong Kong, *na*. Her husband is a banker there and she has all these diamond rings and bangles-shangles made in Chinese factories and then comes and sells them here in Lahore. Very modern and trendy her jewellery is. But despite of that, she told me that in Hong Kong it wasn't selling as well as before. Because of big economic slum that's come there *na*, Chinese have become misers. They think diamonds are luxuries. Stuppids!

But in Pakistan, by grace of Allah, her business is blooming. Because for us, *tau*, diamonds are necessity, *na*. For instant, your daughter-in-law has baby boy. You don't give her diamond earrings she immediately becomes angry and goes off home in a huff. *Chalo ji*, your son's home destroyed. You get your daughter married, you don't give her mother-in-law diamond bangles, she immediately sends your daughter home. *Her* marriage finished. So for happy family life, like food and water, diamonds are must.

Anyways, *all* of Lahore was there at Café Aylanto. At least three hundred people. Sunny, Baby, Faiza, Nina, Natasha, Maha, were all there, wearing designer *joras* and carrying big, big handbags with lots of buckles and zips and fringes and

119

studs and all. Totally fab. They were trying on the jewels and going "*hai* Allah, how *cute*," and posing for pictures for *Good Times*' photographer.

And guess what? Madam Mulloo was there. At first *tau* I thought I should do total ignore and act all cool and all but then I thought, I damn care. So I made a bee-hive for her and asked her what her cousin fundo Farva was giving her for helping her to unload her dwarf daughter on us. She acted all innocent-type.

"*Haw*, what am I hearing?" she said. "I suggest my rich, young cousin for your aged, bald, die-vorced cousin and you say this to me?"

"At least my cousin's not four-foot-eight and nor does his father slaughter sheep with his own hands on his driveaway. And besides my cousin didn't make his money yesterday and that also doing shady export."

"What are you suggesting, *ji*? If you want to say that my cousin's husband is a drug smuggler then why don't you just come out and say it?"

"Okay, *ji*, he's a drug smuggler."

"*Haw*. Look at you! Saying such mean, nasty things about an honest, God-fearing Muslim. Who told you to say them, *haan*? And besides, nice coming from you, whose own aunty and uncle robbed the central revenew with both hands for I don't know how long."

"At least they didn't do it in drugs. And just because you act all holy, don't think I don't know what goes on in your home."

"What do you mean by that? *Haan*? Tell?"

I was about to tell her about her daughter, Irum, who I've heard is roaming around with a cheapster shop-*wallah* type who has no bagground and no future prospectus either but just then the *Good Times* photo-*wallah* came near us and Mulloo and I immediately turned to him and putting our arms around each other, smiled at the camera. The minute he moved away, we jumped apart to pick up the fight where we'd left it, but Sunny and Maha came to do whispered gossip and say how much Faiza was buying and from where was she getting the money when her husband's bottled juice business had dried up so much he couldn't even pay his employees, *haan*? And Sunny said, maybe that Senator Carry who is bringing all this American aids from America, is also giving her some.

"It's for us civilians this time," she said, "not for army. Army's been hogging all the aids for ever but now it's our turn."

And then when the girls left I looked around for Mulloo to pick up the fight again but the coward, she'd left. She'd snaked out when I wasn't looking because I think so she was afraid that I would beat her in the argument. Bubble and Sunny showed me the lockets and rings they'd got and I thought to myself why am I not buying? Am I any less than them? So I also bought small cute diamond locket and then I hid it in my bag because I couldn't tell Janoo. He disproves of nice things like diamonds and emeralds and gold and every time I buy some jewellery he says how much more do I need. He is very bore like that. I think so he must be having some Chinese blood from somewhere.

30 *October*

My and Mullo's fight has been dissolved. She admitted that Farva had promised to ask her husband, Sheikh Ilyas, to help her husband, Tony, with a car dealership if she found a nice boy for Tasbeeh quickly. Now that she's finished her studies and her *nikah* is also broken, Tasbeeh's just sitting at home and ageing and Farva is so worried, so worried that she's saying prayers five, five times a day and getting sheep slaughtered left, right, and centre, to get Tasbeeh married off quickly before people start saying that she's a left-over. And so Mulloo said that please couldn't Jonkers just marry her. Tasbeeh'll get such a big dowry. House. Cars. Servants. Jewellery. Plots for more houses. Foreign exchange in numbered accounts in Swizzerland also. And Tony would be so grateful—his sanitary towel business has also gone *thup na* because of the slum—and if Jonkers could do Tony this small, little favour then he'll almost gift Jonkers a brand new Honda salon to displace the one Miss Shumaila took.

So I said to Mulloo that Tasbeeh was nice and all, but one thing: she was too much on the short side.

"She'll wear heels," said Muloo. "Platforms are so much in fashion."

She also didn't do any talking.

"Once she's married she'll talk and talk. I give you guarantee."

And Farva was bossy.

"I'll ban Farva from visiting."

What about the sheep slaughtering?

"They'll become vegetarians. And you know, they might even give Tasbeeh a flat in London."

"*Haan*," I said, "knowing them it's probably in Eeling-Sheeling or Southall or some poor place in the back of behind." I know all these cheapster Pakistanis who show off about their flats in London and then you discover that they are in Hound Slow or Hack Knee or some place where you wouldn't even send your servants for a holiday—should you ever give them one.

"No, no, their flat is in Knightsbridge. Two streets from Harrods. Four bedrooms. Lying empty all the time. They never go. Can't bear to leave their country for one second even. Except to Saudi for Hajj of course."

"Don't lie."

"I'm not lying. It's true. I swear on Irum's head."

"Near Harrods?"

"And Harvey Nicholas. And also Pak embassy, in case you lose your passport."

And then I thought about how I have to beg Janoo every summers about renting a flat in London so I can also go and do my little London trip, like Sunny and Maha and Faiza do, and how much fighting we do over it when he says no he wants to do a safari instead—as if there aren't enough beasts in his own family. Sometimes he wants to go to some bore place like Cambodia to see temples—look at him, as if we were Hindus off to do *puja*—and I have to beg and beg. Now I'd have my own place, well, almost, and that also on the backside of Knightsbridge. How jay Sunny would be. How Faiza would burn with envy.

So I called Jonkers and I said that he should think again.

"But Apa, you said her father was a drug smuggler."

"Who knows who smuggles what, Jonkers? It's not nice to be so judging. Maybe he's just a *seedha-saadha*, honest-type smuggler who only smuggles nice things like Bosh washing machines and Samsonnight suitcases. You can make good money with that also, you know."

"But what about the girl herself? You said she was a mouse and that she was completely under her mother's thumb."

"Maybe it was just a not so good day for her, Jonky. Maybe she got shy in front of us. Or maybe she'd just seen a sad film. I remember after I saw that Indian film *Paa*, you know in which Amitabh Bachchan is a little boy with a big bald head, I remember I was depress for a whole week. Maybe she's also too sensitive like me. Otherwise *tau* she's probably, you know, real joking laughing type."

He was quiet for so long after that I thought he'd hanged up.

"Hello, Jonkers? Have you gone?"

"Apa," he said at last. "I'm sorry but I have to ask you something. Please don't get angry, but is there something in this for you?"

"Meaning?"

"Please don't mind my asking, but are you being bribed?"

"*Haw*, Jonkers! Bribe? *Me*? And after everything I've done for you. Imagine! You saying such a thing . . . to your Apa."

"Look, I'm sorry but just the other day you were saying that they were completely different to us and the mother was a bully, the father was a criminal, the house was ghastly, the girl was hopeless, the servants were shabby, the food inedible. There wasn't a single thing about them that you liked. Except that they were loaded but even their *crores* couldn't make up for their lack of background. And now you're saying that the father's straight and the girl is the life and soul of the party and no doubt you'll say in a minute that the mother's a delight. And if I needed any further proof that the girl's not for me, it's my mother's wholehearted approval of the family. I don't expect my mother to look for anything other than money, but you're meant to be looking out for my soulmate. I'm sorry but I smell a rat."

"What rat-shat, *yaar*? You don't want nice house and cars and servants, *haan*?"

"I already have a house. And servants. And a car."

"No you don't. Miss Shumaila took it."

"I've bought another."

"And you have flat in London also? On backside of Harrods, *haan*? Where you can go and stay the whole of summers and do shopping all day, all night? That also you have?"

"So *that's* the lure. The flat in London."

"Girl is not bad also, Jonkers. She's quiet, mediocre type. Like you wanted. All she needs is a make-out. I'll get her a fab new wardrope and Loubootin platforms and then I'll take her to Nabeela's and she'll give her a fab haircut and pluck her eyebrows thin, thin and put highlights—"

"Apa, if there's one thing that my marriage ought to have told you, it's that I'm not looking for money."

"Jonkers, you are crack."

"Besides I want to tell you something. I've met—"

"I'm not interested." And I slammed the phone.

31 October

Today is Holloween. Kulchoo's been invited to a fancy dress
party thrown by the daughter of General Shaheed Bull.
General Bull is owner of Punjab Chemicals. They have huge
house on Main Boulevard with fifteen-foot walls outside with
barb-wire on top. Just the kind of people Kulchoo should
be making friends with. I shouldn't say this because he's my
son but unfortunately, Kulchoo is becoming antisocialist
loser—just like his father. He won't go to the Chemicals
party because he says it won't be a good scene. So I told
him the scene would be very nice because Sunny tells me
the floors are of Italian marble and there are fountains inside
and—

"Not *that* kind of scene," he groaned.

"Then what type scene?"

"The social scene. You don't know the kind of kids who'll
be there."

"I know them. They are all nice, rich children from nice,
rich homes."

"Yeah, right. They're all obnoxious, rich kids who get high
on coke, and then go looking for a *phudda*."

"So who's asking you to fight with them? You sit on one

side talking nicely and if they offer you Coke, you say no thanks, I'll take Fanta."

"Jeez, mum, not *that* Coke. Forget it. I'm going to Farhad's house. More my thing."

See what I mean about antisocialist loser? Farhad's father has a small business doing land-escape gardening. His mother does dramas in the TV about bore, bore things like honour killings and child marriages and female infanty-side, all the unpatriotic things that give bad impression about us to foreigners. She wears cotton saris and her glasses on a string round her neck and her hair in a grey bun. Bore NGO-type, if you know what I mean. And they live in a small house near the Ganda Nala. Farhad wants to be an artist. Not a business magnet, not a politician, not a general but an artist. Loser. He makes these big, big paintings with cartoon-type people fighting with sticks against really loud, gody yellow and red baggrounds and Janoo says they are clever and witty but I think so they are useless.

Last time Farhad was here I asked him why he didn't make nice scenes of fields and trees and clouds in greens and beiges that matched my curtains and sofas? That way he would become Lahore's top artist because all my friends would buy. But before he could make a reply, Kulchoo grabbed him by the arm and said, "Farhad, *yaar*, come and see this fantastic new computer game I've got," and pushed him out of the room. I don't know *where* Kulchoo's manners have gone. Honestly.

I said to Janoo, last year we were invited to three Holloween parties and this year we've only been invited to one. Why are there no more witches' and monsters' parties this year? And Janoo said it was because everyday life had become a waking nightmare. Why wait till 31 October, when horror was being visited on us every day? And I said to Janoo, I said, "Janoo, I think so you need to go on Prozac."

1 November

I told Janoo about Jonkers' refusal to marry fundo Farva's dwarf daughter. Janoo said we should all give three chairs for Jonkers. And I said that Jonkers was biggest crack in Gulberg, if not Lahore. And that he, Janoo, was crack number two. He said no, I was the one who was crack for even getting involved in people's marriage proposals in the first place and how did I know who would suit Jonkers and who wouldn't and couldn't I find something better to do with my time? *Uff, aik tau* I'm so bored of that lecture of his. Honestly, he's doing time-wasting sewing wheat and cotton on his lands. He should be a schoolmaster. But then I wouldn't have married him because you can't even buy one Mulberry wallet with a schoolmaster's pay.

So I said to him, "What is better than helping people find happiness? I'm better than you who just sits and rats and raves about the world's problems. And, besides, it is a duty of all Muslims to help others find happiness. Ever since ancient times in Mecca good Muslims have been doing it."

"And ever since ancient times good Muslims in Mecca have also been riding on camels," said that traitor Kulchoo, who was also sitting there. Father and son laughed like hyenas and said maybe I should sell my air-conditioned Toyota and buy a camel. To be like good Muslim of ancient times.

And then I said loudly, "Listen to me, Sheikh Ilyas and Farva are *seedha-saadha*, honest—"

"Sheikh Ilyas, did you say?" said Janoo. "The Sheikh Ilyas of the betting syndicate and gold-smuggling ring? The same Sheikh Ilyas who, a couple of years back, when things got too hot for him, took off for Dubai for several months? That one? I wouldn't be surprised if he's wanted by the law-enforcing agencies of several countries. No wonder he's ready to bestow the London flat on Jonkers. He probably can't go near it himself."

For two full minutes, I *tau* passed away in shock. Look at Mulloo. Doing this to us. She's always been so greedy. Thanks God I found out in time. But between you, me, and the four walls, I *tau* immediately knew Farva and all were bad news the second I slapped eyes on them. First expressions are always right.

"So, Mum, when can we meet our new smuggler cousins-in-law?" asked Kulchoo. "Do they have four-wheel drives with smoky windows? And a white house? With white columns and a dome? And barbed wire and spiky glass on their walls?"

"Ask her if Sheikh Saab has gold teeth," whispered Janoo to Kulchoo, plodding him on. "And if the wife wears a gold bullet in her navel."

"Shut up, you two. And for your information I didn't meet Sheikh Saab. He wasn't there."

"So the rest is all true? The white house, the four-wheelers, the—"

"I'm not talking to you both time-wasters," I said and pounced out of the room, with my nose in the air. Even after I'd shut the door, I could hear their laughter down the corridor. Stuppids.

2 November

Thanks God I've finally found a new maidservant. Her name is Ameena. I stole her from Faiza. I knew that Faiza gave her eight thou a month so I offered her five hundred more (I sent her a message through Faiza's driver who is a cousin of our driver, Muhammad Hussain) and so she immediately dropped Faiza and she came. Just look at these people. They don't even have this much of loyalty.

Nice thing about her is that she's all trained and everything. Knows which clothes have to be hung and which folded. Which shoes go with which clothes and so on and so fourth. Basically, she knows how to talk, how to walk, how to be. Isn't a stuppid, illitred villager. So I won't have to kill my brains teaching her everything from snatch.

I called Mummy and told her that I'd got a new maid to replace that she-snake, Jameela.

"See, I told you Allah takes with one hand and gives with the other. Name?" asked Mummy.

"Well, Mummy, you know He has ninety-nine names. Which one do you—?"

"No, no, the maid. The *maid's* name."

"Oh, *her.* Her name's Ameena."

"She can't be called Ameena."

"She *is* called Ameena."

"Well, she can't stay Ameena. You *know* Ameena was my aunt's name. My father's only sister. Change her name. Call her Shameem or Naseem or whatever. But I won't have a servant in your house called by my aunt's name. It's rude to my aunt's memory."

So I called in Ameena, sorry, Shameem and said, "From now your name is Shameem."

"But my name's Ameena."

"Listen, I give you eight thou five hundred. Your name is Shameem."

Ameena's cheeks blew up for a bit after that. But I think so she'll get used to. She'd better.

Then I said, "I haven't done your interview."

Just then Jonkers called me on the phone.

"Apa, may I speak to you?" he asked.

"Whenever you want, Jonkers. Except now. I'm in middle of an interview." And I put the phone down.

So Am—Shameem said that I'd been seeing her for the last four years whenever I went to Faiza's place. I must be knowing her by now. I told her that seeing was all very well but still there were some things I needed to know about her. So she said what did I want to know. I asked her if she knew any foreigners. She looked a bit surprised but she said no. Next I asked her if she had any rellies working in Abu Dhabi or Dubai or Oman or Saudi or any of those sandy-type places. Again she looked taken back and asked why I wanted to know but I said, "You just answer, *ji*." She said her cousin had once gone to work on a construction sight in Dubai but he'd died there in an accident and after that no one had gone from her family.

"Very good," I said. "And now tell me, is your mother alive?"

"No, she died three years ago."

"She's not likely to die again, is she?"

Now she looked at me as if I'd really gone crack. But I damn care. I'm not getting stabbed in the back again by a sharpie maid.

Just as I finished my interview Kulchoo came in, all sweaty and red as a tomato in the face.

"*Hai Allah!* What's happened to you?" I said. "Are you having a heart attack?" Mummy told me you sweat a lot when you have a heart attack. "Ameena, I mean, Shameem, go quickly and call Muhammad Hussain to the car. I'm taking Kulchoo Saab to the hospital." And I grabbed my bag and stood up.

"Mum, I've just done three laps of the park," panted Kulchoo. "I need a cold drink, not a stretcher."

Oh thanks God! Honestly, the sooner Jonkers gets married the better. Otherwise *tau* my nerves will shatter.

9 *November*

Today there was a knock on my bedroom door and when I said come in, who should come in but all the servants: cook, bearer, sweeper, gardener, my driver, Janoo's driver, Kulchoo's driver, guards, maid. They all came in a group to say that they wanted a raise in their pay.

"*Haw*, why?" I asked.

"Because price of sugar has gone so high and we can't afford."

"So who's asked you to eat so much sugar? It's bad for your teeth. You should hear my dentist. He's forbidden Kulchoo from drinking sugary drinks. Coke *tau* is a total no-no. You know how many teaspoons of sugar it has? Ten. *Ji haan*. Ten. I'm telling you, you don't want to pay thousands and thousands to fill cavities. Besides, also, you'll get diebetees. *And* sugar puts on weight. Ask me, it's been a year and I'm still trying to get rid of those five pounds I put on from eating all those ice creams and chocolate cakes in America last year."

They all looked at each other and then Muhammad Hussain who's been with us the longest said, "Bibi, sugar is the worst but prices have become too much in everything—*daal*, rice, *atta*, electricity, gas, petrol. We won't be able to pay our children's school fees if you don't give us a raise."

136

"So put them inside my husband's school, it's free."

"My village is two hundred miles away from Saab's village," said the cook.

I don't know why these people can't move. I'd go tomorrow to Dubai if you sent me. I think so they have no spirit of adventure.

Muhammad Hussain cleared his throat. "So, Bibi, what is your decision?"

I wanted to tell them that listen I also have to live, okay. Who's going to pay for my hairdresser, my spa, my tailor, my waxing woman, my jeweller, my kitty, if you're going to eat me alive? Money doesn't come out of taps, you know. But they don't understand these things. They think we are made of money. Always wanting, always asking. Never doing *Allah ka shukar*. Never satisfied.

"Okay I'll speak to Saab when he comes," I said to get them off my back. "But I'm not making any promises."

Janoo, of course, immediately said that we should give them all a rise. And that we should have given them already. *Aik tau* he's also such a softie. I said how about giving me a rise also? If you think sugar has gone up you should see how much gold has gone up. Only yesterday I was asking Shazad at Goldsmith how much a ten-*tola* necklace costs now and the reply he gave almost made me pass away with shock. But of course Janoo never ever thinks of my needs. Sometimes I think so I would be better off if I was his driver instead of his wife. Then he'd have a guilty conscious about me and give me a rise whenever I asked.

10 *November*

Tomorrow is our kitty day again. Thanks God, I'll get a brake from Aunty Pussy and her constant demands. Honestly, she's drunk up all my blood. Anyone else in my place would have told her long ago to get lost. But me, I'm too gentle for my own goods. Mummy says I've always been like that. When I was small I wouldn't squat flies with a big thump like everyone else but instead I'd do it gently, slowly with four, five little taps. *Haan*, so where was I? Oh yes, the kitty.

This time it's Sunny's turn. We've thrown Nina out, *na*. She was going around everywhere saying how we'd eaten her money and she was giving us a bad rep, so we decided to give her her money back. So there's just the nine of us left. And because Sunny lives near Raiwind, which is in the back of behind, Mulloo's asked me for a lift. Irum is taking her car for tuition, she said. They, poor things, have only one car left now, *na*. So poor they've become. Well, they have two but the other one's a tiny Suzuki that everyone keeps for servants to get vegetables and meat from the bazaar and not even Irum is prepared to be seen in *that*.

You know, *na*, that ever since Tony's business went bangrupt, Mulloo has been depress. The banks have been asking for their money back and they've had to sell a plot they'd bought in Cavalry Grounds for Irum's dowry. Mulloo puts out a brave face but I think so the sich has been bad in their home. For instant, they sold their sport car ages ago and then I saw some diamond studs at Goldsmith which had come for selling. I was ninety-five per cent sure they were hers but you know Shazad Goldsmith, he never says. Even though I asked him to please tell *na*, and promise by God, swear on Holy Koran won't tell anyone, he just said they belonged to a client. So *pukka* he is.

And also Irum's roaming around with a poor type. Kulchoo made me swear I wouldn't tell anyone, and particularly Mulloo because she *tau* doesn't suspect anything at all, but he said the boy is a DVD-*wallah*. These children, they know every-thing about each other. It seems to me they can't even go to the toilet without telling everyone on the computer. And sending photos also. So Irum's boyfriend has a DVD shop called Kool Kat, probably on the backside of some small pathetic-type market. And nothing else. No house, no name, no family, no lands, no industries, no *uggla pichhla*, nothing. Just a stack of DVDs.

And Mulloo, poor thing, is hoping, no, not just hoping, counting on Irum to make good marriage to a nice, rich type. Also she'd love to migrate to Canada and live in Missy Saga which Baby says is just like Gulberg, it has so many Pakistanis. It's so *desi* that the number of *darses* and other Islamic meet-ings that take place there don't even happen in Lahore, Karachi, and Isloo combined. But I don't think so Mulloo and Tony can leave because Tony is in too much trouble.

He made two fatal mistakes, *na*. When he was doing well, he was openly rude two times to his bank manager who at that time *tau* drank down his anger but now that Tony's a defaulter and the bank manager's sister has just got married into the family of the Interior Minister, the foot is in the other shoe. So Tony and his family's name have been put on the exit control list. Mulloo pretends that she stays here for the love of her country but it's really because she can't even enter the International Departures section at the airport.

And I also know that in the quiet Mulloo does some catering from her house. Provides food to Zeenat's schools' canteens. I know because the woman who runs the canteen there is my waxing-*waali*'s sister-in-law. And my waxing-*waali* also does Mulloo, so she knows. And so I know. But Mulloo doesn't know that I know. Mulloo puts money into the kitty from there only—from the *biryani* and *naan kebabs* she makes. Naturally, she doesn't want anyone to hear even a whisper of it because she doesn't want people to know how poor she's become. She even hides it from me but I know because when I've called her, the maid's said that Begum Saab's in the kitchen. And not once, not twice, but at least three, four times.

We all have friends who have nice German kitchens full of stainless steel and mixers-shixers and American fridges and they sometimes go into those kitchens to do some non-smelly cooking like baking a cake or, as they say, fixing a salad (as if it was broken or something). But no one, absolutely no one, goes into the greasy kitchen in which servants cook the daily food. I mean, why would they? And you know what? Mulloo doesn't even have a smart kitchen. She only has the greasy servants'-*wallah*. So she goes into *that* and cooks. Imagine! And something else also. Since I first started suspecting, I've smelt *zeera* on her. And once or twice onions even. Raw.

And when everyone of her age is applying to American colleges for more studies, Irum's not. One, *tau* Tony can't afford and two, Irum, she's not very serious-minded, *na*. As Kulchoo says she's not scholarship material. But then nor is her mother. And father *tau* poor thing is total loser. I guess brains are not in Irum's jeans. Not like Kulchoo who gets from both sides.

You know, *na*, that Kulchoo came top in his class in his mid-term exams? I distributed cake among the servants and called Sunny and dropped it casually into the chit-chat. Just to make her burn because of all the boasting she does. Janoo of course didn't say anything except "Well done, Kulch." But coming from him even this much of praise is like Noble Prize.

I told Janoo, "See now, how good tuitions are?"

"You mean *despite* all those mind-numbing tuitions he did so well," he said. "Imagine how he'd do without them."

I thought to myself, no point arguing with cracks. So I didn't say anything more. All I want now is for Kulchoo to get into a top college, or at least better than Sunny's, Baby's, Nina's, and Faiza's children, and to not get snatched by some sharpie, greedy girl before he leaves. Then I want him to come back and start big business and make big marriage and have big family. Every night before I go to sleep I say one small prayer for that. "Please, *Allah Mian*, keep my Kulchoo safe from snatchers."

You know *na* that low-class-type girls are always trying to grab innocent, up-class boys with sobbed-stories about how they live only for them and how they will die without them and so on and so fourth. And before the boys even leave for college they've dug their pointy nails into them and got them to agree to an engagement and before you know it, *chalo ji*, they've got your son.

So the other day Kulchoo's friend Kashif was over and they were sitting with me and Janoo and doing chit-chat and then they left together to go to Main Market. Two minutes after they left, mobile rang. It was Kulchoo's Blueberry. Normally *tau* he never ever forgets it anywhere. As Janoo says, it's like apart of his body, like his leg or arm, and can only be removed by armputation. Anyways, I picked up. Before I could say hello even, a screechy low-class-type shrieks in my ear, "Kay, you promised you'd call at three and now it's seven past three. If you've found someone else just come out and admit, okay?"

"Who are you?" I asked.

Silence.

Then the screechy voice says, "Who are *you*?"

Look at her! Questioning *me*. As if I was a servant. "His mother only."

Again silence.

Then: "Where's Kay?"

"Out. Who are you?"

"Nobody."

"Well, open your ears and listen to me, Nobody. Leave my son alone. Otherwise nobody will be worst than me. Understood?"

And I banged the phone down. Well to be frank, I couldn't bang because it was mobile, but you know what I mean. And then I flung myself down on the sofa and howled, "*Hai* my poor baby, Kulchoo. Where've you gone and got stuck up?"

"What's happened?" asked Janoo, peering out from behind his newspaper's wall.

"It's Kulchoo!"

"Is he okay? What's happened?"

"No," I moaned. "He's not okay. He's lost."

"What *are* you going on about?"

"Kulchoo's having an affair."

"An *affair*? Isn't he a bit young for an affair? The boy's just fifteen."

"I just spoke to her on the phone. Voice like nails on blackboard. Low-class. Urdu medium accent. I can just imagine her. Thin, scrawly thing with padded bra and false eyelashes tittering around on scuffed stilettos. *Hai*, my *bacha*, what have you gone and done?"

"Relax," said Janoo. "It's probably just a phone romance. It'll blow over in a month. You should be glad he's normal. He'd have to be gay if he didn't think of girls."

"*Kulchoo's a gay?*"

"All I'm saying is that it's perfectly normal for a fifteen-year-old boy to show some interest in girls."

"But not girls like that, that slu—"

"Shh, quiet."

There was the sound of footsteps coming and I heard Kulchoo's voice outside the door. I quickly put the phone down on the table between us. It lay there like a loaded gun. Janoo held his finger up to his lips and gave me warning scowls. I sat hands in laps. Eyes on table. The door opened. Kulchoo and Kashif came in.

"*Ye lay* Kashif *yaar*," said Kulchoo, seeing the phone on the table. "Your phone." And he picked up the phone and tossed it to Kashif.

"B-but isn't that your Blueberry?" I asked Kulchoo.

"Nope. Mine's right here," Kulchoo patted his back pocket. "Blackberry. Not Blueberry."

"It can be Strawberry now, for all she cares," laughed Janoo.

"No missed calls?" muttered Kashif, staring at his phone.

"Nobody called, *beta*," I said with a big smile. "Absolutely nobody."

11 November

Yesterday was such a bad day, such a bad day that don't even ask. In fact, it was worst day. Honestly, I'm *tau* giving a thousand, thousand thanks that I escaped with my life. I should have known that it wasn't going to be a good day when that crow thing happened in the morning. As I was walking to my car, a crow that was sitting on a wall suddenly scooped down and did number two on my head. Luckily I was holding a newspaper over my head at that time because sun was very strong and I didn't want to become tanned. So thanks God my blow-dried hair didn't get spoiled. People say it is a good amen when a bird does potty on you, but I'm sorry, what's so good about your head being used as a toilet?

So I arrived at Mulloo's house and sent my driver, Muhammad Hussain, to ring her front-door bell. The minute the bell rang, Mulloo sprang out of the front door like a jock-in-the-box. She was wearing a big grin and a new, bright pink silk *jora*, sleeveless to show off her fat white arms and even pearls round her neck. Between you, me, and the four walls, she was looking a bit over as if she was going to a big lunch, but still I wished I'd also worn something else instead of my usual two-carrot diamond ear-studs that everyone has seen a thousand, thousand times.

"*Wah*, Mulloo," I said when she got into the car, "you're looking very dressed-up."

"I thought I'd make an effort today," she said, smiling. "It's my turn, *na*."

"Turn?"

"To take the kitty."

"Oh *haan*. I *tau* completely forgot. What are you going to do with it?" I'd spent mine on two designer *joras*—plain, simple ones for small dinners-shinners. One was from Karma and one from Body Focus. Because I'm fair-minded.

"I think I'll buy some things for Irum's dowry. You know bed-sheets, towels-showels, things like that. But obviously not local. From foreign." And then she saw my face and added quickly, "Normally of course Tony takes care of all these things. But I begged him this time to let me do it. 'Let me do something useful for once,' I said. I'm so bored of spending on designer bags and even more jewellery. After all, what am I going to do with yet another diamond ring, hmm?"

I wanted to tell her to show me a jeweller's where you can buy a diamond ring with a hundred thou (no, ninety thou, because Nina's dropped out) and I'll show you a cheater. But I didn't. Because I'm not like that.

The talk at Sunny's was all about the Butt–Khan wedding. It's over, *na*. Didn't even last two weeks. The girl side says that the boy is a prevert. He asked her to do things on their wedding night that you wouldn't even ask someone from the Diamond Market to do. Everyone wanted to know what type things but Sunny said she couldn't say because she'd sworn on her children's heads. (Sunny is Shabnam's lady-in-waiting, *na*, and she does all her social work for her, like defending her rep, putting out gossip about her enemies, blowing her strumpet, announcing what she gives to charity and so on and so fourth.)

"Dirty things," Sunny said, "*very* dirty things."

And the boy side are saying that the girl is rigid. You know, cold. At least that's what Faiza said. Faiza is not exactly the Khans' boot-licker but she is Ruby Khan's class fellow from their Sacred Heart Convent days and she goes and stays every summers in their flat in London for free. Anyways, according to Faiza the girl doesn't like the bedroom side of marriage. Things became quite heated between the two of them because each started arguing as if it was for their own child while everyone else said that they always knew the marriage wouldn't work and why hadn't anyone asked them first before doing the proposal.

In between, my mobile rang. It was Jonkers, asking if he could see me some time because he had something to tell me. I thought to myself that oh God, it's bound to be sobbed-story about how his mother bullies him and how he misses Shumaila, so I said, *haan*, *haan* of course Jonkers, nothing I'd like more, *yaar*, but right now is not a good time because I'm in the middle of a very important discussion. I'll call back.

As soon as I put the phone down I completely forgot Jonkers and gave myself up to the goss about the Khans and the Butts. And I must admit, I *tau* enjoyed myself very much because I thought serve Shabnam right for being such a meanie to me. Wearing her gody necklace and treating me like I was some maid or something. She'd got her just desserts. Of course I didn't say because, to be frank, her husband is still important, *na*, and you don't want it getting back to her. And then her getting back to me.

But Mulloo, I think so, had the best of times because when all the money was pushed towards her, her face lighted up like a thousand-what bulb. She quickly slipped the money into her purse, shoved the purse deep inside her bag, zipped the bag and tucking it under her arm, said to me, "Ready?"

On the way home along the canal bank we saw all these fruit-*wallahs* parked under the trees with their carts heaped up with guavas and oranges and bananas.

"*Hai*, stop, I want to buy some fruit for my baby," said Mulloo. I wanted to ask her why she doesn't send her cook to buy fruit for her baby like all of us do but then I thought maybe she's had to let her cook go also. So of course I didn't mention. And why? Because I'm sensitive like that.

So I told Muhammad Hussain to stop, but far away from the fruit-*wallahs* because I didn't want any flies coming into the car. When he'd parked by the side of the road, Mulloo gave him some money and asked him to go and get her some bananas and oranges.

"Haggle, don't pay first thing he asks," she shouted at Muhammad Hussain's back. "These people think we are made of money."

You know, *na*, at that time of day there's not so much traffic on that road—the school rush has finished—and so thanks God we didn't have any beggars-sheggars bothering us and also cars were passing in ones and twos. So she put up the window and she turned towards me and I towards her and we settled down to a good old goss about whether the girl was rigid or the boy was prevert when we heard a tap on the drawn-up window on Mulloo's side and without looking up I waved to Muhammad Hussain to put the fruit into the boot. Mulloo also didn't turn around to look at the window but again the tap came so she put the window down and said, "Put it into the back side."

Except that it wasn't Muhammad Hussain but some strange man with a beard, turban, and small, red eyes. Thinking he was the fruit-*wallah* come to complain, Mulloo said, "I'm not paying one *paisa* more, *sumjhay*? So give if you want and don't give if you don't want. You aren't the only fruit *wallah* in the world."

"Open your purse," he hissed, bringing his face close up to Mulloo. Little spots of his spit landed on her cheeks.

"*Hai bhai*, what's the matter with you?" said Mulloo shrinking back.

So then I also looked properly and saw this crack-type with darting eyes and strange pulse tickling in his forehead. He had his head pushed through the open window so his face was only a few inches away from Mulloo's.

"You want me to use *this*? *Haan*?" He half opened the wastecoat-type thing he was wearing and in the inside pocket was a pistol. And not plastic toy like Kulchoo used to play with but real pistol just like they have in James Bond films. Except that this man looked nothing like Pears Brosnan.

Mulloo *tau* froze. Her eyes became wide, her face white as salt. She just sat there clutching her bag to her chest. He reached in and snatched her bag.

"*Hai*, please," she yelped, tugging at his arms.

"Shut up, *kutti*," he said through gritted teeth, slapping her hands away.

I don't know what happened to me then but seeing him hitting Mulloo like that and calling her a bitch suddenly made my blood bubble over.

"Stop that!" I yelled. "You want money? Take the money, but don't you dare touch her."

"You want me to use this, *haan*, you want *this*?" he said to me, patting his wastecoat pocket and scowling at me.

"I'm not scared of you, okay?" I opened my wallet. Luckily there were only two thousand-rupee notes in it. I took the money and flung it at him. "This is all I have. Take it and go," I said.

"Give me the wallet."

"Here!" I flung that at him also. I never carry credit cards, so I reckoned, what do I loose, except a Gucci wallet.

He blinked. I don't think so he had expected me to reply back like that. That made me even more braver.

"Now get lost!" I said.

"Not without *these*," he snarled. He put his hand in and tugged at Mulloo's pearls. For one second, the back of his hairy hand was pressed against Mulloo's throat. Then the string snapped and pearls splattered into her lap. He gathered the string with the few remaining pearls still hanging from it and put it in his pocket. Then he leaned over and grabbed at the pearls that had fallen in her lap, his hands moving all over her thighs. Suddenly his hands slowed down. Then, the bastard, he put his right hand between Mulloo's legs and kept it there, all the while staring at my face. His mouth was open, his lips wet. He was breathing hard. Mulloo sat there as if turned to rocks. His hand dug deeper. I watched in shocked silence. Then someone honked and he looked over his shoulder. I followed his gaze and saw, about thirty yards away, under a tree another man was waiting on a motorbike with its engine running. He was also turbaned and bearded but wearing dark glasses. This other man signed to him to hurry.

"And you," he barked, at last removing his hand and pointing at me. "Give me your rings and earrings."

"The ring is stuck on my finger. I can't get it off. See for yourself."

"Wish I had a knife so I could take your finger off. Give me the earrings! Hurry! Before I tear them out."

Slowly I began to loosen the screws at the back of my earrings.

The man on the motorbike honked again and made hurrying signs to the man at our window, but more harder this time.

"Hurry up, *kanjri*," he shouted at me.

"I'm doing my best," I said calmly, even though my fingers were shaking and inside I was shouting, "Don't you dare call me a whore, you pimp, you bastard." And then in the car mirror I saw Muhammad Hussain, paying the fruit-*wallah* and turning back towards the car with two bulging bags of fruit in each hand. I saw him frown at our bearded guest, confused. I know from the TV news and from friends to whom these things have happened, that when things like this happen it's always the guards and drivers who get killed. Muhammad Hussain's been with us fourteen years, from when Kulchoo was a baby. He used to carry Kulchoo on his shoulders and whenever he went home on leave, he brought Kulchoo dates from his village. He still does. He's a bit slow and stuppid but he's ours.

"Oh look," I said loudly, budging Mulloo in the side and pointing to a big black Land Cruiser with black-out windows that was coming down the road towards us, "there's Iqbal Bhai's car. He's seen us. Look he's stopping." Inside I was terrified that Mulloo might say something stuppid like "Iqbal Bhai, who?" But thanks God she didn't. She just stared at the approaching car, her chin trembling, her eyes staring.

The man also looked. I didn't know whose car it was but it was slowing down for the speed bumps that are all down that road. It was just the kind of car that drug dealers or big feudals with wandettas in their families have. Cars like these are usually packed inside with bodyguards carrying Kalashnikovs. Drops of sweat broke up on the man's forehead. I prayed underneath my breaths, my shaking hands still at my ear. Mulloo sat like a statue beside me. A statue with silent tears rolling down its cheeks.

The Land Cruiser had slowed down to a scrawl and was just twenty yards away. I saw in the mirror that Muhammad Hussain had finally understood what was happening (I told you *na*, that he was slow) and was running towards our car, the bags of fruit banging against his legs. Please God, I said inside my heart, please don't let anything happen to him. There were two, three honks from the motorbike and an impatient vroom-vroom from its engine. The man looked at the motor-bike, then at the Land Cruiser and then at me. His face became purple with anger. Snarling, he suddenly plunged past Mulloo so that half his body was in the car and tried to grab me by the throat but I flattened myself against my door so that his hands grabbed at empty space.

"Give me those earrings, *gashti*," he shouted.

My one earring was off and now I was really frightened so I held it out to him on my open palm. It lay there like a tiny ice chip. Janoo had given me the studs for our tenth wedding anniversary. Once again the beardo plunged towards me, but when it came to it, I couldn't hand it to him. Just as his fingers reached mine, I closed my fist and quickly put it behind my back. No way was I going to give this bastard my anniversary present from Janoo.

He roared with rage. "I'll kill you, you dirty whore." And he pulled out of the car and tried to open Mulloo's door but I leapt to her side and locked it and zipped up the window. He spun around to come to my side. My heart was beating inside my mouth. I quickly locked my door and got down on to the foot mat and sat there crouching with my arms over my head, praying. Then I heard three impatient blasts of a motorbike horn followed by more vrooming of the engine, but this time quite near to our car. Swearing loudly, the beardo thumped his fist hard on the roof of the car, kicked the tyre, and then, just as I expected him to start firing at my window, I heard his footsteps running away from the car. I put my head up and looked through my window. I saw him leap on to the back seat of the motorbike, with Mulloo's bag under his arm, and roar off in a cloud of dust.

The Land Cruiser with the blacked-out windows, meanwhiles, drove quietly away. Muhammad Hussain pulled open the driver's side door and panted, "Bibi, are you all right?"

I reached across to Mulloo, put my arms around her, and held her close.

12 *November*

If I am frank, I have to admit that sometimes I wonder why I'm still married to Janoo. I mean, between you, me, and the four walls, he's a bit of a kill-joy, no? Doesn't hang up with the cool crowd. Doesn't do GTs unless I drag him. Hates balls. Never knows any gossip. Won't make friends with important types. Totally bore, antisocialist person he is. When he's in Lahore all he does is stay at home reading the papers, watching the news, playing tennis and swimming with Kulchoo, and meeting with just four or five bore types. There's that dinosoar he plays chess with. Then he knows a couple of NGO types in *chappals* and hand-woven *kurtas* and then there are some bore journalists with whom he talks of bore, bore things like geopoltics and Offpak or Afpack or whatever it is. And that's it. Total loser, no?

But then something happens and I know why I'm still married to him. Like yesterday, for instant. When I got home after dropping Mulloo, he was getting ready to leave for Sharkpur. In fact, he was already sitting in his Prado jeep. He got out to say goodbye but when he saw my face he told the driver to take the luggage out. He wasn't leaving that day.

And then he took me inside and held me in his arms while

I shaked and shaked and in between shaking told him what had happened. He asked me only two questions: did I take the number of the motorbike? No? Never mind. He'd check with Muhammad Hussain. Was it a *jihadi*-type terrorist or just a common criminal? I told him he had a beard and turban and that he called me a whore and he touched Mulloo and that he snatched her pearls and wanted my diamonds and I don't know if he robbed us to fund the *jihad* or to just buy himself a motorbike but *why does it matter?* Janoo held me close and stroked my hair and said, "Shhh, shhh, I know, I know, I'm sorry," and then he gave me a Lexxo (he normally disproves of trankillizers because he says I should do yoga instead but I guess so he thought what had happened to me wasn't normal) and he tucked me into bed and sat holding my hand till I fell asleep. He was still there when I woke up two hours later. While I was asleep he called up everyone he knew in the police and guvmunt and God knows where-all to trace that motorbike. But as usuals, of course, no luck. The only times terrorists get caught in this country is when they attack generals or other army officers. Otherwise when they attack ordinary people like us or even not-so-ordinary people like Benazir and Murtaza Bhutto, they get off spot-free.

And he also said I was very brave and that he was proud of me and from where I had got the courage to stand up to that bastard but if, God forbid, anything like this ever happened again, I must never do such a thing again because it could be dangerous. Things like money and jewellery, he said, didn't matter, these things come and go. But I mattered. I mattered a lot. When I told him that I didn't want to live here any more and could we please move to a place where we could be safe, he fell silent and looked at the floor. Later he said to me that if we were to move, I would always miss this place. It was our home and without it we'd be homeless. I said I damn care. And he said, "But you *would* care, believe me you would."

Later Mummy came to see me and she did so much nice fussing of me and Aunty Pussy came with pastries from Punjab Club and Jonkers brought a huge, expensive buffet of foreign lilies and he did total ignore of Aunty Pussy when her lips became thin at the sight of the foreign lilies.

Even through my upsetness I noticed that Jonkers looked different. His old General-Zia-type glasses had gone. And without those heavy black frames and thick glass you could see his eyes properly. They were like a camel's, all big and dark, with lashes as long as my curtain fringes. I asked him if he'd had his eyes lasered and he gave me a sheepy smile and nodded. "I took your advice," he said.

"Eighty thousand it cost," sniffed Aunty Pussy.

And one more thing: he was wearing jeans and an apple-green polo shirt. I wanted to tell him how cool he looked but didn't in case Aunty Pussy commented about the cost of his clothes as well.

Baby also came to see me and Nina came and Sunny came and Faiza came and they all came with money for charity to take off the evil eye that someone had put on me. And they all said how lucky me and Mulloo were that the beardo didn't do anything worst to us. No one said it then, but we were all thinking of how sometimes they rape and shoot women just for wearing sleeveless or not handing over their money quickly enough. *Hai*, and even my shweetoo Kulchoo who never gives me any praise, said I was a cool mum. And I overheard him boasting to his friends how I had fought off a terrorist.

Me and Mummy decided to visit the local mosque afterwards. It is four streets behind our house. That's where all the servants go to pray on Fridays before lunch. Or they say they are going, but God alone knows what they do when they leave the house. I think so that they pretend they are going but actually they sneak back to their quarters to have a rest. They are like that. Sneaky. *Haan* so where was I?

Yes, the mosque. Me and Mummy actually wanted to slaughter a sheep as a thank-you to Allah for my safe escape and also to take away the evil eye that had been put on me. But because it is harder to hide a sheep in the house (we couldn't let Janoo find out, *na*, otherwise he'd go up in bloom of smoke and call me illitred and uneducated and supercilious and God knows what all) so we thought we'd give some money for charity instead. But again we couldn't tell Janoo we were going to give it to the mullah in the mosque because he is also anti them, *na*. He says they run *madrassahs* where they take poor boys who have no choice and make them into suicide bombers while they send their own sons to nice schools and get them jobs in multinationalists. I think so Janoo is a bit polaroid, between you, me, and the four walls. The money in the mosque just feeds the children of poors who come to learn the Koran there.

We waited in the car while Muhammad Hussain went inside to fetch the mullah. When he came out he was a youngish man wearing a beard and turban just like my attacker. (The mullah, not Muhammad Hussain.) As soon as I saw him, my heart came into my mouth again and a loud buzzing started up in my head. I didn't want to give the money to him but Mummy said to me in a whisper, "Looks bad now." So I handed over the money but I was careful not to let his fingers touch mine. Nor did I look at his face.

15 November

I went to see Mulloo today. I hadn't seen her or even spoken to her on the phone since that day with the beardo. Sunny, Nina, Baby, and all, when they came to see me they said that they'd dropped in at Mulloo's also but Tony had said she was resting and wouldn't let them go in. And she hasn't called anyone after that. Not even me. In fact, Mulloo has dropped out of the social scene altogether. No one's seen her, no one's heard of her, nothing.

So when I arrived at Mulloo's place, Razia, her maid, told me that Mulloo Begum Saab was resting in her bedroom and I shouldn't disturb her or she'd yell at her and maybe even throw her out of her job. I said doesn't matter, I'll make her keep you again. And I pushed past her into Mulloo's room.

At first I couldn't see anything because the curtains were drawn up but when my eyes became used to, I saw this lump-type thing in the bed under the sheets. I switched on the lights and the lump threw off the sheet and started screaming, "Razia, I *told* you not to bother me. Get out. Fool! Idiot!" It was Mulloo.

I said to Mulloo did I look like Razia to her and why wasn't she getting up? She sat there on her bed with her hair all wild, wild and her eyes all crazy, crazy, looking at me as if she'd never seen me before and I swear I thought she'd finally cracked. The room was also smelling as if no one had opened the windows in a month. So I pulled back the curtains and threw open the windows. She immediately pulled the sheets back over her head again and started moaning and rocking like a weepy rocking horse.

"Come on, Mulloo, *yaar*," I said. "It's not the end of the world, you know."

"It's fine for you," she sobbed from under the sheets. "You didn't lose ninety thousand and your pearls also. And you didn't have him touching you. He *touched* me! I feel dirty."

"I know, Mulloo, and I'm really sorry. But it's over, *yaar*. And we are both alive and we haven't been raped even."

"Yes, it's over. Everything's over for me."

"*Haw*, Mulloo. How you can say this? The pearls and money were just *things* and Janoo says it's okay to lose things."

At that she flung back the sheets and glared at me. "It may be okay for you and your darling Janoo but it's *not* okay for me. Do you know how hard I work for my *things*? Do you have *any* idea?"

I went up to her. "Don't be like that, Mulloo."

"Go away," she shouted, flapping her hands at me as if she was shooing away a crow. "Just go away and leave me alone."

"Listen to me, Mulloo," I said, sitting down on the side of her bed. "I know it was scary and I know that man touched you and took your pearls and money, and he didn't take so much of my money, nor my diamonds, but he also threated *me*, you know, and he also called me dirty names and he was going to kill me if the other one hadn't taken him away just then. If I become depress and stop talking to my friends then I will let that man win. But if I keep living like before and I keep going out and being myself, then I win and he loses. No?"

"Everything for you is a game," she laughed emptily. "Isn't it? Winners and losers. Well, I don't want to play."

She pulled the sheets up and disappeared under them again. As if I wasn't there.

"Mulloo?" I said.

"Go away. Leave me alone," she shouted from under the sheets.

"Mulloo—"

"Get out!"

"Okay, Mulloo, then I'll go."

As I walked to the door she called out, "Listen, please don't tell anybody what he did to me."

"Of course I won't, Mulloo."

"Swear, swear on your child's life."

"I swear."

Outside the door I met Razia.

"Where are Tony Saab and Irum Bibi?" I asked her.

"Out," she shrugged.

"Tell them to stay with Mulloo Bibi. She needs them around."

"Can you keep me yourself?" She tugged at my sleeve. "I don't ask much. Only seven thousand. That's all. Please? I can do waxing and threading also. Okay, six thousand five hundred for you."

I shook her hand off my arm and walked straight away past her.

16 November

As if we didn't have enough problems, now we've even got dengue fever. Honestly! And I thought that only poor countries like Africa got it. I'm so worried, so worried that my poor darling Kulchoo is going to get it. Yesterday when he came home from school I told him he's not to eat street food from roadside stalls and he's not to drink water in other people's houses because God knows if they use bottled or drink from taps only and he's not—

"Why?" he asked.

"Haven't you seen how much dengue fever there is?"

"But what's that got to do with food or water? Dengue's spread by mosquitoes."

"Oh?" I said. "Is it? Well, don't go near mosquitoes then. And, even if there are mosquitoes around don't let them bite you, okay?"

"Take a chill pill, Mum. It's hardly as if I go paddling in ditches of stagnant water."

Take a chill pill! If he knew what I know about Aunty Pussy . . .

So yesterday I had the whole house sprayed from top to bottom with mosquito-killer spray. I also had lots of those green coils burnt whose smell mosquitoes don't like. And also in every room I had those tablets put inside the switches which make the buzzing sound that drives mosquitoes crazy. I also put a net around Kulchoo's bed and I told all the servants that I would fire them if they opened Kulchoo's windows one inch even.

When Kulchoo came home from school he said, "What's that awful chemical smell everywhere?"

"Mosquito spray, and mosquito coils, and mosquito tablets," I said.

"Jeez, Mum. You don't have to go at them with WMDs. I don't know about dengue fever, but by the time you're through, I'll be dead of chemical poisoning."

"Don't speak like that!" I said.

And then he went upstairs to his room and two seconds later I heard him shouting, "Who put these wussy net curtains around my bed?"

Honestly! He doesn't even have this much of gratitude. It's all Janoo's fault of course, for teaching him to question me.

Talking of teachers, I'd gone to a dinner at Sunny's. Janoo had come with me because I've told him I feel scared riding in a car by myself and also if I don't go out and meet my friends and see the world I might go crack like Mulloo. Because I've had a trauma *na*, that's why. I think so he believes me, poor thing, because now he comes quietly wherever I say. I think so I'll keep it up for another five, six years at least.

Anyways, we were at this dinner. Not very big. Only about twenty people. As usuals men sitting on one side of the room drinking whisky and discussing politics and women sitting on the other side of the room drinking Seven-Up and vodka and doing *gup-shup*. Dinner hadn't been served yet because it was only a little bit after eleven o'clock. I felt like doing bathroom and also checking out Sunny's new paintings that she'd bought behind my back from the NCA degree show. She'd told me she wasn't going because "*Bhai*, who can be bothered to go all the way up the Mall with all the suicide bombs and those bore lawyers protesting every day just to see some silly paintings and besides, I've heard this time the show is not so good even." So then when I'd said, "Okay then I won't go also," she'd quietly got into her car and gone. Double-crosser. Back-stabber. Hippo-crit.

So I got up from next to Faiza and went to the toilet. I came out of the toilet and was walking slowly towards the sitting room looking at the new paintings in the corridor— between you, me, and the four walls, they were quite mediocre because Sunny, poor thing she has no tastes, *na*—when suddenly I heard Zeenat's voice. I quickly ran behind a pillar and hid. And then I heard Shaukat's snarling laugh and then Sunny saying, "Come, *na*, please come into the sitting room. So how was the Chief Minister's reception?"

I took my mobile phone out of my bag (Prada, what else?) and quickly dialled Mummy. She answered in a sleepy voice. *Aik tau* Mummy is also such a loser sometimes. Going to sleep at 11:20. Imagine!

"Mummy," I said, "it's me."

"I know," she mumbled.

"Okay," I said.

"What do you want?"

"Has Aunty Pussy told Zeenat Jonkers' decision yet?"

"Who? Jonkers' what?"

"Oho, Mummy. Wake up!" And I repeated my question again.

"I don't think so," she yawned. "She was saying yesterday that she's sure Jonkers will come round if we give him more time. Why? What's happened?"

So I told her I was at this dinner and Zeenat was also here and that I needed to know in case Aunty Pussy had said anything. And what was I to do?

"Talk a lot but say nothing, darling. Just bury her under an . . . an . . . ava—, what's that word meaning flood of snow, ava something—"

"Ava Gardner?"

"No, no, not Ava Gardner. Ava Gardner was an actress. Ava something else."

"Avalasting?"

"No silly, it's ava—"

"Mummy I don't want to play this bore word game. Say what you want or otherwise shut up the phone."

"Just give her so many compliments that she can't get one word in about Jonkers or anything else." *Aik tau* Mummy is also such a clever one, *na*. No wonder Janoo calls her Kernel Klebb. I think so she was a famous spy from a James Bond movie. The Kernel, not Mummy.

When I returned to the sitting room, Zeenat immediately patted the seat next to her on the sofa.

"How lovely to see you here," she said, kissing me on the cheek. "Did I tell you how much we all enjoyed meeting you that evening? We must do dinner again soon."

"*Hai*, what a fab *jora* you're wearing, Zeenat Apa," I said, sitting down next to her. "Let me guess. Bunto? Faiza Sammee? Or maybe from India? Sabyasachi? Varun Bahl?"

She looked down at the burnt orange crepe outfit she was wearing as though she'd forgotten what she'd put on. I hate when people pretend like that.

"Oh *this* one," she said. "I've had it for so long that I forget where it came from. Tell me, how's that charming cousin of yours? I thought he was such a fine young man. So gentlemanly, so courteous and—"

"And your earrings," I butted in. "They are looking like real hairlooms to me. No, Faiza? Don't Zeenat Apa's earrings look like *pukka* hairlooms? Look *yaar*, what fat pearls. Basra, I'm thinking. Agricultured ones *tau* don't have this shine at all, no?"

And Faiza also reached over to look and did lots of oohs and aahs and boasted about her own mother's earrings that were also of Basra pearls that she gave to her daughter-in-law who then left her husband (Faiza's brother) but took the pearls and now how their hearts smoke with anger whenever they see her going about town wearing those earrings. Another five minutes passed. I wished that Sunny would serve dinner, so we could snake out quietly. I tried to catch Janoo's eyes across the room in the men's side, but he was deep inside a discussion with Akbar. *Aik tau* Janoo is also such a hippo-crit *na*.

When you beg and beg him to come with you to a dinner, he won't and when you drag him out and then you want to leave, he won't. Honestly.

"Just the other day Tanya was saying to me how much she'd like to meet you again," said Zeenat, touching my arm.

"*Haw* look at her, what a liar!" I thought to myself. And then I said: "Faiza, have you seen Zeenat Apa's house? So much art she has, that don't even ask. And all modern, modern, trendy, trendy."

So then Faiza, who is a shameless show-offer, talked for ten full minutes about her own art collection and how all of Lahore's top artists do so much respect of her and how they are always saying that no one knows about art like she does and Zeenat kept trying to cut her off but once Faiza starts only Al Qaeda can stop her. So in that time I again tried to make signals at Janoo. But would he look at me for one second even?

When Faiza finally stopped, Zeenat turned to me and said, "Shall you, me, and Tanya have lunch some time next week? And maybe you could ask your cousin to join us too?"

Haw, doesn't she have any work to do? Who runs her schools, *haan*, if she's out lunching all the time? What a fraud. And between you, me, and the four walls, I'd rather have lunch with Mullah Omar than that rude daughter of hers.

"*Hai*, I'd love to," I said, "but you know next week I think so I'm going to Sharkpur with my husband. It's our village, *na*. Spending one week every month there is *tau* total must for me. We run a school there, my pet project. But it's small and for poors only. Charity. Not big business complexed like yours, of course."

"How admirable. When are you back from your village?"

"I don't know yet. Maybe this time we'll stay for whole month."

Thanks God then Sunny finally announced dinner and before Zeenat could say anything else to me I escaped into the dining room. I got there first and everyone must have thought I was such a greedy but I damn cared. I managed to escape her during dinner also. Every time she came near me, I quickly made an excuse and went to the other side. Thanks God it was standing-up and not sitting-down dinner or otherwise I would have been trapped next to her. Once I said, "Oh, look at that salad. Beatroots are my best vegetable. Must have *na*." And then, "You know something, I'm *tau* just dying for water. No no, I'll get it myself. I always do all my own works." And third time I even went into the bathroom and stayed there for five full minutes but then I thought what if people outside think I've got cholera or something because this is second time I've been and so I quickly came out and thanks God by that time desert was being served and like it always happens, as soon as everyone had put their desert spoons down, they said *Allah Hafiz* and thank you very much and everyone left altogether.

On the way home Janoo said to me, "I understand you're coming to Sharkpur with me next week. To check up on *your* pet project."

"If you heard it from Zeenat, just ignore. You know, what

she said to me? That Tanya was dying to meet me again. Look at her! She's such a liar, that one."

"She's not alone," said Janoo in a tired-type voice. I looked sideways at him but he was looking straight down the road. What did he mean?

17 November

I called up Jonkers and I said to him, "Listen, Jonkers. You've got to tell your mother to tell Zeenat Kuraishi that you don't want to marry her daughter." And then I told him what had happened to me last night. He listened quietly and then he said, "I'm sorry you had to go through that. I'll make sure she calls Zeenat and tells her."

Then he said he wanted to talk to me and that he'd called a few times but that I'd always been busy. He said that in fact he had to ask me a favour but that I mustn't tell anyone. Whenever someone tells me I mustn't tell something to anyone, immediately my ears start tinkling with excitement because I know, I just know, I'm going to hear some delish, *garam masala* gossip. And also I immediately start thinking, now who can I tell it to?

So I said cross my heart and swear on the Holy Koran and please tell *na* and he said did I remember the girl we saw at Shabnam Butt's daughter's wedding? We saw no girl, I told him. We did, he said. She was dressed up in yellow *shalwar kameez* and she stopped his mother from falling. He'd been trying to tell me for the longest time. Her name, he said, is Sana and he'd followed her that night and made enquiries about her and discovered that she was an old school friend of Shabnam Butt's daughter from the time that they were at the Convent of the Holy Family. Shabnam and all were not so rich then and didn't send their daughter to Lahore Grammar like all the old-rich of Gulberg and Cantt do now. In my time, we— the rich, old-family-types—used to go to Convent of Jesus and Mary. Only middle-type people used to go to Holy Family. That's why their daughter must have been together with this Sana person. Anyways, he said he had to go now but could he take me out to lunch soon because he wanted to tell me something and also remember, I mustn't tell anyone as yet. What bore gossip. Not even worth passing it on to anyone else. Typical Jonkers.

In the afternoon Mulloo came to see me. I was in my bedroom getting a padicure when she burst in looking like an unmade bed. Her hair was all messy, messy, her clothes all crumbled, her eyes swollen and she smelled like old laundry.

"*Haw*, Mulloo," I said, "what's happened, *yaar*?"

"Send her away first," she said raising her chin at my padi-cure-*waali*. Honestly, it was a bit much of her asking me to get rid off the padicurist when Mulloo knows that she charges five hundred an hour and that I had nail polish on one foot and not on the other. I wanted to say to her wait five minutes, let her paint my other foot also but then I saw Mulloo's trembling chin and her beatroot face and I thought no, better do as she says or else she will make a scene. So I gave a big sigh and paid the padicurist and she left grinning like Tony Blair. User. See if I ever call her again.

As soon as she was gone Mulloo threw herself on the sofa and started wailing like a ghost from the graveyard.

"I'm ruined," she sobbed, "finished."

"Has something happened to Tony?" The bank manager must have taken him off to jail, I thought. Or maybe he's having an affair. Tony, not the bank manager. Maybe he's also put a girl from the Diamond Market in a little house in Defence and has been feeding her with Mulloo's earnings from her *biryanis* and *kormas*. Or maybe he's done another *ghupla* and he's been caught with his hands inside the cash safe. You never know with men, *na*.

"It's Irum," she cried. "She's gone and fallen in love with a DVD-*wallah* and she says if I don't agree to a marriage she will run away with him. With a DVD-*walla-a-a-h*! What have I done to deserve a DVD-*wallah* with a shop in Defence? *Haan?* I've kept my fasts, said my prayers, done my charity, even gone on Umra twice and this is how Allah repays me. With a DVD-*wallah*! He gives everyone else banker sons-in-law and feudals with thousands of acres and IT millionaires with green cards and I get a DVD-*wallah*!"

She picked up one of my hundred-dollar silk cushions that I got from Singapore last summers and pressed her face into it. I thought of her fat tears and her greasy hair and her running nose and I considered for a minute offering her a local cotton cushion instead but then I thought she might tear up my cushion, the mood she was in.

Otherwise I didn't know what to say. If I said I knew from before only about the DVD-*wallah*, then she would say why didn't I tell and she would accuse me of laughing behind her back. And if I pretended I didn't know and she found out later that I did, then?

So all I said was, "*Haw*, look at Irum," while looking at my one unpainted foot. And then to make her feel better I said, "But you know, Mulloo, ever since all these bombs-shombs have been bursting all over the place, people have stopped going so much to cinemas. Instead everyone's staying at home with DVDs to watch on their own private home cinemas. The DVD shop-*wallahs* must be making so much money. Who knows, this man might be a DVD millionaire even? *Haan?*"

"Don't be stupid. There's no such thing as a DVD millionaire."

"You never know *yaar*—"

Suddenly she grabbed my knee. "You've got to save me!"

"*Haw*, Mulloo—"

"Please have a proposal sent for Irum. Only you can do it."

"But from *who?*" I was *tau* non-pulsed.

"From your cousin."

"Which cousin?"

"Jonkers."

"*Jonkers?*" I screeched. "Mulloo, he's thirty-seven. Irum's *sixteen*. And . . . and he's bald and he's sober-type and he's diè-vorced. And he's not even that rich, you know."

"But at least he's not a DVD-*wallah*. And he's foreign-returned and he is comfortable and he has his own business—"

"So does the DVD-*wallah*."

"We know your aunt and uncle also."

"You can also get to know DVD's mummy and daddy."

"So you want me to marry off my Irum to a DVD-*wallah*?" she asked coldly, flinging my Singapore cushion on to the floor.

"I'm only saying that just because you know someone's mother and father or because they are foreign-returned you can't marry your child off to them." I picked up my cushion and put it back on the sofa out of Mulloo's reach.

"And what," she said, raising her eyebrows at me, "did *you* look at when you went searching for a wife for your cousin? *Haan?* Just that you knew the girls' parents or, even worst, knew someone who knew their parents? Just that, *na?* You even went to look at Tanya Kuraishi. I know all about that so don't try and deny, *ji*. And also you went to see a girl who's in love with someone else. And by the way, both of them are in their early twenties so don't give me lectures about age difference."

"Is Tasbeeh in love with someone else? *Haw*, Mulloo, what a traitor you are! Imagine sending us to do a proposal and not even telling us this much."

"So are you going to ask your aunt or not?"

"Who's she in love with?"

"The DVD-*wallah!*"

"Even Tasbeeh?"

"No stupid. Irum! What do I care about Tasbeeh?"

I looked at Mulloo properly. Her eyes were crazy and her breaths were coming so fast that she looked like she'd just finished a ten-mile run. I knew then that she was not in her proper mind. So instead of arguing with her I began asking her how she'd found out about the DVD-*wallah* and Irum. And she said that she first became suspicious when Irum's phone bills became more than their electricity bills. And then she started listening at doors and things and before the week had finished she'd found out.

So then I gave her some tea and when she'd drunk two full cups and calmed down a bit, I said to her that Irum won't marry anyone else as long as she was in love with her DVD-*wallah*. Mulloo asked what she should do and I told her if you don't mind I'll send for my Mummy. She knows answers to everything like this. Mulloo agreed to let me call her but only on one condition: that she has to swear on my head that she won't tell anyone, not a single person. I wanted to tell her that she can't attach strings like that to Mummy. But I said, don't worry, my Mummy is tight as your fist.

So while Mulloo sat, I sent the driver for Mummy and she came and she also had two cups of tea while she listened to Mulloo's story with narrow eyes and then she said best thing was not to get Irum married to another man but to get her to fall out of love with this one. And best way to do that was to invite him to their house all the time and start calling him *beta* dear and doing twenty-four-hour flattery of him which will make him very pleased with himself and Irum very irritated with him. And then she said, Mulloo and Tony should even start criticizing Irum in front of him. Saying things like, "*Beta*, please explain to Irum not to speak so much on her mobile phone. *Of course*, we don't mind her talking to *you*. Of course you are like our own son, but all these friends of hers, really is it necessary to waste so many hours on the phone with them?"

Mummy said Irum was only throwing herself at him because she wanted to annoy her parents. She said all children do this. He was forbidden fruit but if he became just an ordinary banana or a stinky little guava, then she would get bored of him in two months flat. And also if he started siding with them against her, *then* he would really start gettting on her nerves. Mulloo looked a little doubtful but Mummy spoke in her Kernel Klebb voice and said, "Don't do as I say, Mulloo, and you will regret *all* your life."

"No, Aunty, you are saying right," she said.

"You wait and see, the minute he starts saying yes aunty and no aunty and whatever you say aunty, your daughter will go off him like this." Mummy snapped her thin fingers.

"*Bilkull*, Aunty, you are right. I'll go home and straight away call him for dinner."

When she'd gone Mummy said, "Mulloo really should do something about her appearance. She looks like a sweepress."

I didn't answer because I was checking my Singapore cushion. Honestly! The sacrifices you have to make for friendship.

19 November

Jonkers took me out to Causa Nostra for lunch. On the way there he was wearing snazzy dark glasses, but Jonkers being Jonkers, they didn't have a label. And he was sitting with an arm slung out of the window, like he never used to before. I swear he's changed. Where he used to look all nervous and not-so-sure before, now he looks as if he knows what he's doing and where he's going.

At Causa Nostra on the table next to us were Raheela Hassun and Shazia Hameed. Raheela's husband is Royal Tractors and Shazia's father is Jub TV. Their hair was blow-dried into long blonde curtains and their Versace dark glasses, all studded with gold logos at the sides, were pushed on top of their heads like hairbands. Diamonds glinted inside their ears and on their fingers and their wrists. From the way their heads were joined together, and they were speaking without moving their lips, I knew at once that they were doing top-secret gossip. They looked at me and gave small, fake-type smiles. I also smiled back fakely and reaching behind me, pulled out my maroon Bootega Veneta bag and placed it on the table in full view. My father may not own a TV station and my husband may not be a tractor but still they should know I am not hungry-naked.

178

And anyways between you, me, and the four walls, everyone knows that Royal Tractors are Defaulters Number One who took such big, big loans from the guvmunt. For four months they didn't give one *paisa* even to the poors who worked for them before they closed down their factories and told all those poors not to look at them for money but to go and find new jobs somewhere else and now they say they are hand in mouth and they can't pay back the money of the loans. But we all know they've just bought two flats in Kensington and a villa in Dubai and if you don't believe me just take a look at Raheela's diamonds. And Janoo told me Shazia's father hasn't paid one *paisa* even in tax. And why? Because Shazia's father says his TV channel is public service because all it shows are mullahs answering questions from the public. Questions like will women who wear nail polish go to hell and which side your bed should point so if you die in the night you go straight to heaven. But everyone knows that everyone tunes in and that it is Cobra and Psycho's fave channel and that he gets so much adverts on it that don't even ask.

I wanted to order a big juicy burger with cheese and French fries but then I looked at Shazia and Raheela and they both looked so thin in their skinny jeans, so I ordered a salad and diet Coke and wished they'd speak a bit louder so I could also hear their goss. All the time opposite me Jonkers was talking and talking. I think so Shazia must be doing bitching about her sister-in-law. She's just got married to a hot-shot business typhoon in New York and has a twenty-room sweet in Trump Tower and Shazia is so jay, that don't even ask.

"You'll really like her, Apa," said Jonker. "She's independent and clever and kind. Would you like to visit her office with me?"

"Hmm," I said, not really listening. I'm forgetting Shazia's sister-in-law's name now. She's studied from some university in New York. I think so it's called Columbo. Janoo says it's good. Maybe we'll send Kulchoo there also. But not if it's going to make him a gay.

"Is tomorrow okay, then?" said Janoo. And Raheela, she comes from a not-so-good bagground herself. I think so her father was something in sewage. Anyways she had this *chukker* with this man who owns a sugar mill but when he refused to marry her—because he said girls who slept with men before they married them were bad-charactered—she aimed for his best friend whose father is Royal Tractors and because the friend was a bit simple-minded, she managed to trap him. They got married last year.

The waiter put my salad in front of me. Thanks God it had some cheese in it. Otherwise *tau* I would have had to go home and have lunch again. I think so these women, Shazia and all, they must be eating like snakes. Once a week.

"What time shall I collect you?" asked Jonkers.

"For what?"

"For Sana's office."

"Sana who?"

"*Sana*, Apa. *Sana Raheem*, the girl I've spent the last half-hour telling you about."

"Who's she?" I picked out and ate all the cheese and then

started on the two or three green beans doing *purda* behind the whole garden of leaves that they'd piled on my plate.

"Have you heard a single word I've said all afternoon?" Jonkers put his fork down and looked at me strangely.

"Of course, *yaar*. There's this person called Sana Rehman—"

"Raheem."

"Hmm? Yes. Sorry. Raheem. You know, Jonkers, this salad is all leaves and nothing else."

"Salads tend to be leafy."

"Look, Shazia and Raheela are leaving. Wonder where they're going from here? Do you think I could have a burger now that they've gone? You know Raheela's had so many injections put into her face, she's started looking like the Buddhas in Lahore museum. All smooth and peaceful and stony. *Haan*, so this Sana Raheem, who is she exactly?"

"She's the woman I'm going to marry."

The leaf I was swallowing became like a cactus tree inside my throat. I coughed and choked and felt as if I was going to die. Jonkers came round to my side and trumped me on the back and then made me drink a glass of water. When I got my voice back I croaked, "Does Aunty Pussy know?"

"Not yet."

"Who is she?"

"You never listen, do you?" He sighed and then started telling me about Sana all over again.

Apparently this Sana of his, she is twenty-eight years old and works in a travel agency. Her mother is a schoolteacher. Oh no, I thought inside my heart, why do you always have to go for the poor types? She had a father also, but he died in a car crash seven years ago. Father, Jonkers said, was a bank manager but after his death they started becoming poor and so Sana, who was at college doing her MA in English, dropped out and took a job in a travel agency. And mother went to work in a school as art teacher and mother is still art teacher but Sana has become the manager of her agency.

"She's doing really well. You should see her. She's so efficient and calm and—"

"Jonkers, don't mind my asking but how much do you know her?"

"I've met her a few times. Remember my friend, Asad? His wife is friends with her. They were the ones who told me about her at the wedding and they introduced me to her then and later I asked them to invite me when she came by and so they did, twice, and then I dropped by at her office once on the pretext of buying a ticket and then a couple of times since then."

"So you've met her four times?"

"More. And we talk on the phone every evening. I feel as if I've known her for years."

"Like you knew Shumaila." The minute I said it, Jonkers' face crumbled and I felt bad with myself but facts are facts, no? I mean, here I am moving heaven and hell to find him a girl, going to corrupt politicians' weddings and even drug smugglers' houses, all to find him a decent bride from a decent bagground and here he is, again dating secretaries and all. Okay, I admit travel agent is better than a blow-dryer but still, *yaar* . . .

Jonkers wiped his mouth carefully with a napkin and put it down on his side plate. Then he said, "I know, Apa, you look down on women who have to work for a living but your attitude is both outdated and, if you don't mind my saying so, unpleasant. I realize Shumaila probably married me for my money but she was only trying to do the best she could for herself. And you know something? In that, she was no different to those two ladies who were sitting at that table, or indeed any of your wealthy, well-connected friends who marry rich men just for their wealth."

"*Haw*, Jonkers, what have I said? You *tau* are getting after me for nothing."

"Look, I'm sorry. But I know what you're thinking. Travel agent equals glorified secretary equals gold-digger."

"*Never*. Never in a thousand years. Cross my heart. Honestly, Jonkers, what do you take me for? *Haan?*"

"So will you come with me to her office? I'd like you to meet her. We'll have to pretend you're buying a ticket. I'd have liked to have introduced you properly without these silly excuses but I can't just yet. I don't want to put pressure on her. I know she's the girl for me, but if she needs more time, she must have it. So will you come?"

"What do you mean, she's the girl for you?"

Jonkers' face broke out into an enormous smile. "When you meet her, you'll see."

"Have you told her?"

"Not in so many words but I suspect she has a pretty good idea. I'm prepared to wait. I'll wait twenty years if I have to."

"No, you have to get married in one month's time. Before Muharram."

"What do you mean? Why?"

"Because Aunty Pussy . . . never mind."

"So will you come? Next week?"

"Okay, let me think. I'm not saying yes, just thinking."

"Please don't mention this to my mother just yet. I don't want her barging in like a crazed bull and scaring Sana away."

"So you're never going to tell Aunty Pussy? Don't mind, but you're not going to do another Shumaila on her, *haan*? Marrying in a mosque behind your mother's back and then bringing your bride home for breakfast."

He laughed. "I can't see Sana agreeing to that. She wouldn't sneak off and get married without telling her mother. They're very close. And in any case, Sana has a lot of pride. She'd never go for a hole-in-the-corner thing like poor Shumaila did."

"Hmm," I said, but inside my heart I was thinking how stupid Jonkers was. How trusting. All of this pride thing this Sana of his is putting on is just an act. The minute she sees his house and set-up and all, she'll change her mind in two tricks.

"Now how about a burger?" asked Jonkers. "That salad looks really miserable."

Hai, shweetoo Jonkers. He's so sensitive.

"Okay *yaar*," I said, "I'll come and see your trav— . . . your Sana. And don't worry, I won't tell Aunty Pussy. But one thing: my coming along to her office doesn't mean I'm okaying your marriage to this girl. Just now I'm only seeing. Also if Aunty

Pussy finds out from someone else and starts chewing my head and saying I knew all along, and why I didn't tell her, I'll just deny, okay? I'll tell her, 'I swear, Aunty, I *tau*, knew nothing.' And you'd better not say anything different." And inside I said to myself, "And she'd better not do anything to my Kulchoo."

20 *November*

Sana's office is on Jail Road, in a big, glassy skyscrapper. I had thought she'd sit in a tiny hole of an office on the back side of Moon Market or something with two peon-types working with her, but no. She is inside a skyscrapper on Jail Road next to Lahore's trendiest furniture showroom, Zamana. But thanks God she is on the ground floor. So no need to use lift. I *tau* feel so scared of lifts. What if electricity goes away when you are inside? Then what? Anyways, her office has big glass windows and marble floors and plotted plants and is all air-conditioned with lots of big desks full of phones and computer screens and lots of people sitting at the desks in suits and ties and talking in English.

As I was walking in I noted that Sana's office has six security guards sitting at the entrance, all carrying Kalashnikovs with belts full of bullets strapped across their chests. Now that the bombs-shombs have become so common, every big office on a main road has double, triple security. Hotels *tau* even have soldier-types in helmets crouching behind big machine guns in little room-type things made of sand sacks at the entrance. At first I was pleased to see so many guards in Sana's office. Thanks God, I thought, if some crazy *mullah*-type bomber comes in, they can kill him then and there only. No questions asked. But then I noted that one of the guards had a beard and he was giving me these funny, funny-type looks. I swear my heart started racing like a camel on drugs. It suddenly donned on me then, "Who will guard the guards?" But then I said some prayers under my breath and I blowed the prayers on me and Jonkers for extra protection and then thanks God that guard yawned, scratched his privates and looked away and I started breathing again.

Sana's desk was bigger than everyone else's and placed to one side and you had to go up a step to reach it. So she sat higher than everyone else.

Someone was sitting with her already, a big feudal type in a starched white *shalwar kurta* and big black moustache that curled up at the ends. So me and Jonkers, we sat down on the sofa placed besides the step leading to her desk and waited.

While we waited, I checked her out. Her complexion was wheatish. On the darkish side of wheatish, to be frank. Aunty Pussy's always wanted a fair-skinned girl for her Jonkers and Irum may be only sixteen and also poorish and Tanya may be a gay and Tasbeeh poor thing may be deaf and dumb, but at least they're all fair. I wouldn't say Sana is double of Aishwarya Rai but she's not ugly either. Long nose. Big mouth and dimples. Hair up again in a high pony-tail. No jewellery. Just a thin gold chain around her neck. This much I will say: at least she didn't look like a Shumaila type. No plunging neckline, no over make-up, no tight polyester outfit, no cheapster jewellery. But then, I reminded myself, looks can be receptive.

Look at Jameela. She always looked so grateful, so polite, and see what she did.

Jonkers was sitting next to me pretending to flicker through a travel magazine. But his one foot was tapping the floor and I could feel the tension coming from his body almost like heat-waves. Today he was wearing an open-necked white linen shirt and casual khaki trousers. He looked as if he was reading but I could tell that all of his attention was fixed on Sana.

The feudal was speaking loudly and jabbing his finger across Sana's desk at her. But as his voice got louder and louder, hers remained same: quiet, calm. The feudal stood up, placed his palms on her desk and leaning across, shouted, "You screwed up. Because of *your* incompetence, my son had to wait for six hours at Dubai airport. *Six* bloody hours!"

Sana didn't shrink. She met his eyes and in a quiet but hard-type voice asked him to sit down. The feudal ignored her. Jonkers flung down his magazine and stood up. I tugged at his trouser leg to stop him—you never know with feudals, *yaar*, they may have gunmen waiting outside; after all, not all of them are decent, peaceful Oxen types running charity schools like Janoo. But he shook my hand off and in two strides he was at her desk.

"Is everything okay, Sana?" he asked, staring angrily at the feudal. The feudal glared back. I said a prayer under my breaths. Please, *Allah Mian*, don't let there be a *phudda*. Because the feudal would make minced meat of poor old Jonkers. I looked around me. There was a small glass-topped table lying by my side. If the feudal grabbed Jonkers, I'd pick up the table and crash it onto the feudal's head.

"Yes, everything's fine, thank you, Mr. Ahmed. Why don't you have a seat on the sofa over there while I explain a few facts to Mr. Shah here?"

"Are you sure?" asked Jonkers, still eyeing the feudal.

"Quite sure, thanks." I could see Jonkers wanted to still hoover by Sana's desk but the look she gave him made him return reluctantly to the sofa besides me. Thanks God. Never knew shy old Jonkers had it in him to behave like Shahrukh Khan.

"So you see, Mr. Shah," Sana said to the feudal in her cool but hard-type voice, "your son had to wait six hours because *he* missed the flight I'd booked for him. I have all the paper-work here. This was his flight, EK01, departing Dubai for London at 11 a.m. He had a confirmed reservation. Business class. I'd even had his seat allocated, as you can see here. But he showed up *after* they had closed the flight. He called me from the check-in desk in a panic and demanded that I get him on to that very same plane. I tried but as I said, the gate was closed by then and as you probably know, they are very strict at Dubai airport. Not like here. He'd also rubbed the Emirates people up the wrong way by making some bizarre accusations so they weren't in any mood to oblige him when he demanded a seat on the next flight. So when he called me it wasn't easy to find him a seat—business class, again—on the next available flight but I managed. The flight was meant to leave two hours later but unfortunately there was a delay because of security concerns and it didn't take off for another four hours. The wait, I'm afraid, was unavoidable. I'm sure if you ask him about the circumstances, he will explain. Meanwhile I'll give you a photocopy of his old ticket as well as the new reservation I made for him and you can look through them at your own leisure."

The moustachioed man snatched the papers out of Sana's hand. Then he turned around and marched out. On the way out, he threw dirty looks at Jonkers and me. Me and Jonkers, we both glared back. Cheapster. Who did he think he was?

After that Sana called us up to her desk. One thing I will say for her. Her father may have been only a branch manager of a bank—and that also a local bank—but she is full of confidence. Not for a minute did she look scared by that feudal. Jonkers had told me that I had to ask about tickets to America. He said that she wouldn't like it if I said I'd just come to check her out. "She's not a prize cow, you know," he'd said to me, "and she won't like it if we treat her like that. So we must make up a story."

"Are you okay?" said Jonkers to Sana. "I'm sorry about that rude man."

Sana shrugged. "No big deal. I come across them all the time." And then she smiled at Jonkers and added, "But I appreciate the concern." Then she looked at me. "Hello, I'm Sana Raheem. I'm sorry you had to wait."

Jonkers introduced us and told her that I wanted to enquire about some flights.

"Sure. Can I offer you a drink?" she asked me. "Coffee? We do good cappucino here. Or would you prefer something cold? Some iced tea perhaps?"

"Coffee please," I said.

"And for you, Jehangir?"

"Same," said Jonkers, with a goofy smile.

She gave the order on her inner-com and then she asked, "Right, what can I do for you?"

"Er, I want to go to America," I said.

"Where in America?" Behind her I saw a big poster of the White House and underneath it it said Washington.

"Um, Washington."

"And when were you intending to travel?"

"In summers," I replied. "We always go abroad in the summers. Gets too hot here, *na*. And bore also. Because all our friends also go away to London and Swizzerland and America and all."

"So June? July? You are very organized to be booking your holiday so far in advance. May I ask how many of you will be travelling?"

"Three. Me and my husband and our son."

"And your son is?"

"Kulchoo. Otherwise *tau* his real name is—"

"Sorry. I meant, how old is he?"

"He was fifteen on his last birthday. In May. He's a Taurus."

"So full fare. Just flights or hotels as well? Would you like me to book any flights within the US also or just to Washington and back? And would that be business class or economy?"

I looked at Jonkers and gave him a small frown. Why did she have to ask so many questions? Honestly, so nosy. Next she'll be asking me my bra size.

Sana caught my frown at Jonkers and looked from me to him. Another thing I will say about her: she's sharp. Just like Jameela was.

Jonkers cleared his throat. "My cousin's here to make some, er, general enquiries. She wanted to have an idea of what's out there. She doesn't necessarily want to book just yet. Isn't that right, Apa?"

I frowned at him again. How many times have I told him not to call me Apa? Stuppid. Now she'll think I'm seventy.

"Yes," I said, "that's right, *Jonkers*." I bet he hadn't told her his pet name is Jonkers. From the way her lips twitched I could tell I was right.

Jonkers' face flashed red.

"So you'd like to fly into Dulles?" asked Sana.

"Washington, not Dallas," I said. She might be sharp in some ways, but in others this girl was quite simple-minded, really. Poor thing.

Jonkers coughed and flashed again. Must be embarrassed for her.

Sana nodded at me and said, "Of course. My mistake."

The drinks came. The coffee was very nice. All hot and fluffy.

"The coffee is very nice," I said. "And office also."

"Thanks. Glad you approve."

"You're not having?" I asked.

"What? Coffee? No, I have to restrain myself because with the hours I work, if I had a coffee every time a client had one, I'd be climbing the walls."

"And going all the time to toilet also," I added.

"Yes," she laughed, "that too."

"So how long do you work?"

"I'm here by nine and leave around six, sometimes seven. But luckily I live close by so I'm home in five minutes."

"Where do you live?"

"Canal Park."

"Oh," I said. Canal Park is a not-so-nice area of Gulberg. Small plots, tight houses, hardly any gardens. But *chalo*, at least it's Gulberg and not Ichhra.

"You work too hard," said Jonkers.

"But I enjoy it," she replied. "And it makes me relish my holidays all the more."

"You must be going abroad on all your holidays?" I asked.

"I wish!" She laughed again. "But our last holiday was quite special. It was my sister's tenth birthday so I managed to get a great deal on a holiday in Langkawi, in Malaysia. We swam in the sea, did some snorkelling, diving, I even organized a guide to take my sister, mother, and me on a short trek through the jungle. It was fantastic," she sighed. "We saw gibbons and hornbills and the most amazing butterflies, big as my hand, and trees so tall they seemed endless . . ."

Maybe that's why she's so dark. All that swimming-shwimming totally ruins the complexion, *na*. Maybe in another six months, she'll be fairer and then Aunty Pussy may even be prepared to look at her. If not, we'll just have to take her to my spa-*waali* and ask her to do micro-dermabasement on her face. But thanks God, at least she's been abroad. She's not a complete villager.

I looked at Jonkers. He had his elbows on her desk, his chin in his hands and was gazing at her goofily, like some character in a Disney cartoon when they are falling in love and their eyes go all dreamy and big red hearts come plopping out of their heads. And this while she banged on and on about bore birds and bore trees. I yawned.

"Sorry," she said at once. "Once you get me talking about nature, I get carried away. Right. Your flight. Would you like to give me your names and some tentative dates so I can start looking for you?"

"Not just now. No, Jonkers?" I said kicking him under the desk.

He woke up from his dream. "Oh? Ya. Sure. Whatever you like. Perhaps it is a bit too early. But *I'll* be in touch with you, Sana. I'll call this evening. Hmm?"

"If you like." Her face became red and bending her head, she started ruffling the already tidy papers on her desk.

"Once me and my husband," I said, "once we've decided exactly when to go, I'll get back to you then. Okay? But thanks for all your help, *haan*. And the coffee."

"No problem. I look forward to hearing from you."

I stood up and started walking out. But Jonkers was not following. I looked back to the desk. They were looking at each other and talking without speaking. Then Jonkers slowly got to his feet. She also stood up. She was his height, same-to-same. Another minus.

All the way home in the car Jonkers ate my head. What did I think of Sana? Wasn't she amazing? Wasn't she friendly?

Wasn't she beautiful? And the way she handled that awful man? Cool, no? So I told him that yes she was nice-ish but also a bit on the dark side and too much on the tall side. And yes she wasn't a cheapster like Shumaila but I told him flat that she still wasn't Aunty Pussy's cup of coffee.

"Not wealthy enough, you mean?" he said. And then he shrugged and said it didn't matter. She didn't have to be his mother's type. She had to be *his* type. Crack.

"Have you forgotten everything I told you about importance of baggrounds?" I said. And then I told him only half the marriage is to your wife or husband. The other half is to their families. And he said that if Sana's family was at all like her, then it would be absolutely fine and he wouldn't mind being married to them at all. But, I told him, you haven't even met them yet. And he said, "Doesn't matter. I have faith." Double crack. I told him that I'd gone and seen Sana because he'd asked me to but that didn't mean I thought she was best thing for him and if anyone asked me if I knew what he'd been up to, I was going to deny, okay? And also that I wasn't doing any pleading-shleading with Aunty Pussy for him.

"Don't worry," he said cheerfully. "Once my mother meets her, she'll come round." Triple crack.

21 *November*

Honestly, life is so tough in Pakistan, *na*, that don't even ask. You have to live here to know. So many stresses and stains. All day, all night. No electricity, no gas, no New Year's Eve and on top everyone is saying the Talibans are coming. Not the Afghan ones who are busy in Afghanistan killing Americans and blowing up NATO trucks but our own home-grown Punjabi ones who are sitting on our heads. And once they come, then *tau* everything will be over. So many times I've heard this now that my head pains every time someone says "Taliban." Let them come, I say. We'll deal with them then. Till then, please don't chew my head off. I have enough problems to solve before then.

Now take yesterday, only. There I was minding my own business, sitting in my own house, doing my own work as I always do, when out of the bloom, my peace was shattered. I was in the middle of taking out my winter's wardrope and putting away my summer's wardrope when my mobile phone rang. Well, to tell you the truth, I was sitting on the sofa in my bedroom putting cream on my feet—Elizabeth Ardent's Eight Hour Cream—and watching Ameena, sorry Shameem, bring up all the suitcases of my winter clothes from the storeroom and unzip them on my bedroom floor and take my clothes out and hang them in my cupboard. I was telling her where to put what when Aunty Pussy called.

"I don't know what's come over Jonkers," she said.

At once I became a lert. "What's come over Jonkers?"

"I just *said* I don't know what's come over Jonkers."

"Oh."

"Do *you* know what's come over him?"

"*Haw*, Aunty Pussy, how should I know? I'm not a smooth-sayer, you know."

"Yesterday he came home in a wonderful mood, smiling and humming to himself even more than usual and being so nice and friendly with me I thought, he looks like he's seeing sense at last. And then he said, 'Please call Zeenat Kuraishi and tell her that I don't want to marry her daughter.' What's come over the boy? Why would he say that?"

"Er, I don't know. Maybe because he doesn't want to marry her. Maybe you should let me tell Baby that he's found someone else."

"*What? Has he?*"

"No, no, Aunty Pussy, it's just a way of getting rid of Zeenat you know. It's better than saying to them that no, we can't marry your girl because she's a gay and rude also."

"We don't have to say anything. It's not done to tell people like Zeenat that you don't like their girl. Best is not to say anything. She'll get the hint."

"But, Aunty Pussy, Jonkers doesn't want—"

"I know," she cut in. "I *know* he doesn't want to marry Zeenat's girl. I'm not going to force him. I've given up on that proposal already. But when I think of that house . . ." And then she sighed and said, "It's already November, you know, and we still haven't found a suitable girl."

"We haven't?"

"You know full well we haven't. Unless, you know something I don't."

"*Haw*, Aunty Pussy why are you always accusing me, *haan*? After everything I've done for you. Going here and there and everywhere looking for a girl. Fighting with my friends for you, arguing with my family for you, telling lies for you. Honestly!" And then I thought, maybe I should tell her about Mulloo and Irum. I know Aunty Pussy won't want but at least afterwards if she finds out through Mulloo or someone she won't be able to say that I hid anything from her.

"Actually, Aunty, there is someone else who maybe you can think about."

"Who?"

"Mulloo's daughter, Irum. She's young, I think so seventeen and not bad-looking. Fair also. Mulloo's looking for a decent boy and when I told her we weren't interested in Tasbeeh she offered her own daughter."

"No! I'm sorry but they're not good enough for my Jonkers."

"Anyways, I've already refused because I didn't think so it was suitable. Just thought I'd tell you, so you knew."

"I'm worried that if we don't find a good girl for him quickly, he'll go and find someone for himself again. Another secretary or a hairdresser. If he hasn't done it already."

"Aunty Pussy, you know, your voice is breaking up. I can't hear. No, sorry, not even now. Still can't. I'm putting my phone down. I'll call you back, okay? Of course I'll do it immediately." And with that I switched off my mobile phone. And also hanged up my landline. And went back to my winter's wardrope and Shameem.

Two hours later I switched on my mobile phone and the second I did, it rang. The number looked familiar but since it wasn't Aunty Pussy's, I picked up. Never know *na*, someone might be calling up with an invitation to a party or at least a dinner.

"You cow. You've stolen my maid, haven't you?" It was Faiza.

"*Haw*, Faiza—"

"Don't you dare '*haw* Faiza' me. I know you stole Ameena. So don't bother denying."

"I don't have any Ameena in my house. My maid's called Shameem."

"Liar! I know you've stolen Ameena."

"Cross my heart and hope to die, my new maid's Shameem. If you don't believe me you can ask all the servants in my house."

She fell silent. Then she said, "Where's Ameena gone then?"

"How should I know?"

Another pause. Then she sighed and said, "I'm sorry, *yaar*. I was sure you'd taken her."

"Who told you?" If it's that bloody Mulloo, I'll go and strangle her with my own hands only.

"No one. You'd said your maid had walked out on you.

Shortly after, my maid went missing. I put two and two together and came up with seven. Sorry, *haan*?"

"No probs, *yaar*. Friends are for forgiving."

I put down the phone and told Shameem that next time Faiza comes she's to go inside the servants' quarters and stay there till Faiza leaves, even if Faiza takes fifteen hours. Okay?

Honestly! So much of stress, so much of tension. I don't know how I survive here. Anyone else would have had a nervous break-out.

23 *November*

Yesterday we went to a GT at Mulloo's. It was small, because GTs are small, *na*. Otherwise they'd be dinner parties. Baby and Jammy, Sunny and Akbar, Janoo and me. That's all. Oh and Mulloo and Tony and Irum also. Because, after all, it was at their house.

Anyways, we walked into their lounge and there was nobody there except this man whom I'd never seen before. He looked youngish, maybe eighteen or twenty with longish hair and T-shirt and jeans and two or three of those colourful woven bracelets like Prince Harry wears and sneakers and no socks. But, thanks God, shaven and with clean clothes and washed hair. Not dirty and greasy-looking, like so many teenagers. He got up and said hello and that his name was Zain and he shook Janoo's hand which was odd because if teenagers greet you at all, they just dig their hands in their pockets and shrug and say hi in a sulky way as if they are being forced to say. Someone had given him a good brought-up.

And then Mulloo came in with an ice-basket and behind her Tony, carrying two bottles of wine and they were both laughing—which was even more odder because I can't remember the last time I'd seen Tony laugh—and they asked us if we'd met Zain. And we said yes and they said he was Irum's friend and Tony clapped him on the back and Zain said, "Here, Aunty, let me," and took the ice-basket from Mulloo's hands and Mulloo beamed at him and then Tony started to ask what we wanted to drink and Mulloo started wondering where Sunny and Baby and all had got to and while all of this was going on, it suddenly donned on me that Zain must be the DVD-*wallah*!

So as soon as I could, I grabbed Mulloo's hand and pulled her down on the sofa and whispered, "Be frank. Is this the DVD-*wallah*?"

"Yes, that's Zain," she giggled. "Isn't he lovely?"

"Where's Irum?" I asked.

"Upstairs, finishing off some homework. She's just coming."

Then Baby and Jammy and Sunny and all came and they started talking about this and that and laughing and joking and through it all I kept noticing that Mulloo and Tony, they looked different, you know, happy. Every now and then they'd give each other smiles. And when Mulloo cracked a joke Tony would laugh the loudest even if joke was limp. When Irum came downstairs she sat down next to Mulloo and sort of smuggled into her side and Mulloo put her arm around her. And every now and then, Irum and Zain would also give each other private-type looks. Which, between you, me, and the four walls, became a bit over and sickish after a while and if it had been someone else in my place they might even have passed some comment about it. But you know me. I never complain.

Because it was just a GT and not a big dinner-type thing,

we were all sitting together, you know, not men and women on opposite ends of the room. And Zain was also sitting with us and talking politics and you know for a poor-type DVD-*wallah,* his English was quite good. And then there was a short pause in the conversation and Janoo asked Zain what he did.

Zain said, "I'm between high school and college but right now, I'm running my cousin's DVD store."

I looked at Mulloo's face to see if she had died of shame, but not for one second. In fact, she was grinning as if Zain had just announced he was a sugar mill-owner.

"Are you interested in film?" asked Janoo. Crack! As if you run a DVD store because you enjoy watching films. I was making signs and symptoms at him to change subject but of course Janoo as usual wasn't looking at me. *Aik tau* he's also such a stuppid.

"Not interested." Zain laughed. *"Obsessed.* That's why I'm doing it. I want to introduce the general public in Lahore to some non-Hollywood directors too."

"Really?" asked Janoo, looking interested. "So who do you rate then?"

Zain wheeled off a list of strange, strange names like Ray and Maal and Four Man and someone else, I think so must be Indian, called Guru Sawa and I don't know who, who else.

"Oh, yes," said Janoo. *"Days and Nights in the Forest, The Seven Samurai.* Excellent, excellent. And Hitchcock?"

"Master of supense," said Zain. *"Psycho* is beyond amazing."

I was about to ask who had made a film about Janoo's younger sister when Akbar butted in and asked Zain what he thought of someone called Score Say Say. And Zain said that he didn't think *The Departed* was his best work but that *Raving Bull* and *Taxi Driver* were "fan-tast-tick." And then Janoo put on a silly face and pointed to himself and said, "You talkin' to me?" in a weird American-type accent and Jammy said, "I'll make you an offer you can't refuse," in a low, horse-type voice.

And they all burst up laughing and started doing hi-fives like silly teenagers and Akbar said but that was Copp Ullah and Jammy said yes, he knew that *yaar*, but that Copp Ullah was better than Score Say Say and that someone's godfather wiped the floor with some taxi driver and they all started arguing, but not in a fighting way.

Then Baby said, "*Bhai*, I know you will all look down your noses at me but I *tau* loved *Omkara*."

"No, no, no," said Zain. "It's *zabardast*. Really, *really* brilliant. Bharadwaj's riff on *Othello*. And the soundtrack!"

"*Dham Dham Dharam Dharaiya*," sang Akbar, and guess what? I couldn't resist joining in. And Irum said she didn't know I had such a nice voice and had I taken singing lessons and Janoo looked surprised and asked if I'd seen this film and I said of course, I've seen every single Indian film that Sound Sensations in Fortress Stadium has ever had and will ever have.

"What did you think of *Maqbool*?" Zain asked me. And then he explained to Janoo that it was an Indian take on Mack Beth.

I said Tabu looked nice with her long hair and long face but that fatty Pankaj Kapoor, I didn't like so much with that big belly of his and really I could see why Tabu didn't want to sleep with him every night. And so I could fully understand why Tabu got Irfan Khan to kill him. In her place I'd have done same. But if I'd had Saif Ali Khan or my favourite Shahrukh or even Amir Khan in Pankaj Kapoor's place, then I wouldn't have looked at Irfan Khan twice. Zain laughed and said "Yeah right," and at the mention of Amir Khan, Sunny said that he *tau* was her total favourite and had we seen *Three Idiots* and of course Janoo hadn't and Zain said he must.

"It's more commercial and bits of it are way over the top," said Zain, "like the birth scene which I'd have chucked out, but still it's interesting. You should watch more Indian cinema, Uncle. Not everything, because a lot of it's still escapist crap but here and there you find some good films. Have you seen *Mr. and Mrs. Iyer*, for instance?"

My hand shot up. "I have!" When all their eyes turned on me, I quickly put down my hand. "*Hai,* so sad, so sad. Those horrid Hindus, you know, what they do to us poor Muslims. But most saddest, their love, unspoken . . ."

"See, you should use Aunty here as your guide," Zain told Janoo. "She seems to have her finger on the pulse of Indian cinema."

"It seems she has," said Janoo, nodding slowly and looking at me as if he was seeing me for the first time ever. Crack.

Zain is such a shweetoo and he has so much of knowledge also. But between you, me, and the four walls, he doesn't seem like a poor DVD-*wallah*. In fact, he almost seems like one of us. If you know what I mean. I think so there's something dishy going on here.

Mulloo called us all in for dinner and one thing I will say for Mulloo, food's always been good in her house, even now she's poor. It was a sitting-down dinner and in the middle of the table was a huge dish of mutton *karahi* with slithers of fresh ginger and spring onion and sliced raw chilli spattered on top and *seekh kebabs* with *imli ki* chutney and *aloo zeera* and *khutti daal* and cucumber and mint *raita* and pipping hot *tandoori rotis* studied with sesame seeds. So we all sat down and tucked in and tucked in and tucked in and no one spoke except to say "pass the *daal*" and "one more *kebab yaar*" and "this is seriously good." And so on and so fourth.

Finally Akbar pushed back his chair, I think so, to give rooms to his belly, and said, "*Wah!* Mulloo, that was the best meal I've had all year."

"Isn't she just the most brilliant cook?" said Zain.

"*You* made this?" asked Baby, raising her eyebrows.

Mulloo flashed and looked a bit uncomfortable. I thought, *haw*, poor thing, now she's been caught. I was about to take pity on her and say something about Kulchoo's tuition to change the subject, when Zain spoke up again.

"You should try her *nihari*, and her *shahi tukras*, and her lemon cake. I've been telling her and telling her to start a catering company like this Pakistani lady did back home in Toronto. She started off real small. Just her and a friend. Now she's h-u-g-e. Huge."

"Fat, you mean?" asked Sunny.

"Uh-huh, she's model thin. And always in designer gear. No,

I meant her business is huge. She has a TV show and she's
written cookery books and she's all over the glossies."

"You live in Toronto?" I asked.

"Yeah. I'm here for six months, till spring, minding my
cousin's store, while he finishes up a project in Karachi."

So he is not a DVD-*wallah*. And he lives in Toronto. And
he probably has a Canadian passport also. And a house in
Missy Saga. It's not fair.

"So, Mulloo, what's stopping you?" asked Janoo. "If I could
get food like this at a party of mine, I'd hire you in a second."
Look at him. As if he throws parties ten times a day.

"Well," said Mulloo, looking uncertainly at Tony. "Tony and
I, we're thinking about it. It's just that . . ."

"Actually," said Tony, clearing his throat in that bore way he
always does before making some bore speech, "Mulloo was
already doing some catering on the side. In fact, she's been a
rock for me these past few months. But the type of catering
she was doing was small-scale stuff. It wasn't until Zain here
started pointing out the potential, that we both looked at it
seriously. I've given it some thought and done some sums and
my mind is pretty much made up. If Mulloo takes on the food,
I'm ready to look after the business side of things."

"Great! Event management," said Janoo, and thumped Tony
on the back. "Good thinking."

"Go for it, *yaar*," said Jammy and he raised his glass and
said, "To Mulloo and Tony's business. May it prosper."

Everyone picked up their glasses and said the same, even
Sunny and Baby, who, if you ask me, were looking a bit

shelf-shocked. And Mulloo still wasn't meeting our eyes but then suddenly Sunny seemed to make up her mind about something and she leaned over and put her arm around Mulloo.

"I book you first!" she said. "For our twentieth-wedding anniversary party in Feb. Can I have this divine *karahi* for it?"

Mulloo nodded and gave her a shaky-type thank-you smile.

"As soon as my A-levels are over I'm going to join Ammi's business full time," announced Irum.

"No, you're not!" said Mulloo at once. "You're going to apply to colleges both here and abroad and go on with your studies. After you finish you can decide what you're going to do. But not one second before."

"*Aw*, come on."

"No come-on, shum-on," said Mulloo. "You're going to college."

"You could always apply to university of Toronto," said Zain, winking at Irum.

Irum flashed, and then gave him a sideways smile.

While everyone was saying goodbyes later, Baby whispered in my ear, "Who's the cute boy?"

"I think so, Irum's friend."

"Mulloo has all the luck!"

24 *November*

This morning I woke up and stretched my legs. They were paining. I stretched my toes. They were paining. I tried to sit up. My head was paining. Then I knew. I was dying of dengue fever. As usual, Janoo had got up at dawn time and gone out. So from my bed only I rang Mummy to ask her to come over immediately with doctor and ambulance. But she wasn't at home. Maid said she'd gone to the bazaar. So I called her mobile and same maid answered and said, "Begum Saab has forgotten her phone at home." Honestly, I think so Mummy's gone sterile. She forgets everything. So then I called Janoo's mobile. He was at his lawyer's office sorting out some property papers or something bore like that.

"Come home," I croaked over the phone. "I'm taking my last breaths."

"What's the matter with you?"

"I have dengue." And I hanged up the phone.

So he came. Took my temperature. And, I'm sorry to say, he did it a bit impatiently. Considering I was dying and all.

"Dead normal," he said, peering at the glass tube.

"But I have dengue," I whispered. "You get pain in your bones when you get dengue. My feet feel like they are breaking and my calves feel like someone has been sitting on them all night. And I'm so tired I can't even lift my head."

"I'm not surprised you're tired. We came home from Mulloo's at 1 a.m. and then you sat up till 3 watching your recorded serial." He got up from my bedside and tripped over my six-inch Jimmy Choose stilettoes I'd been wearing the night before. He held them up and said, "This explains the pain in your feet and calves. Some sensible shoes and a decent bedtime and you'll find your dengue fever will disappear magically."

Stuppid. What does he know? It's not as if he's a doctor or something. Anyways, I was in bed looking after myself because no one else will, when who should come in but Madam Mulloo. She was carrying two huge boxes of chocolate brownies, all done up with ribbon and things, that she proudly announced she'd made herself. The brownies, not the ribbons. She asked what I was doing in bed. I almost said dengue but then I thought maybe it is a disease that only poors get. I mean no one I know has died from it. So I said I was just feeling a bit tired and runned down. That's all.

"Hmm," she said, "you are looking a bit pulled down."

She herself was looking quite, you know, bouncy. Hair blow-dried, lipsticked, scented, walking and talking fast like she used to before. Like the fat, happy Mulloo before Tony's factories ran into trouble. One box of brownies was for me and one for Mummy. To thank us for pointing her in the right direction.

"You know, I was about to lose my mind when I came to see you that day," she said. "I didn't know which way to turn. Everything seemed to be falling on my head. You know, *na*, that things have been a little bit hard for Tony and me? With his business, I mean. Money's been a bit tightish. So I thought, *chalo* never mind, I won't buy so many clothes and I'll cut down on our expenses and help Tony out a bit by doing some catering on the side and I'll make do. And I *was* okay, you know. Not happy, but okay. But then that terrible day happened and that bloody bastard took my kitty and my pearls, and I just fell apart. And when Irum told me about this boy I just thought, now this is limit. Now I'm going to die. But then I came to you and your mother and you fixed it. You fixed everything."

"*Haw* Mulloo, you *tau* speak as if me and Mummy, we were mechanics."

"No really, if you hadn't suggested we meet Zain—"

"You never even told me he lives in Toronto." If I'd known even for one second that he was from there I'd never have let Mummy tell her to call him and be nice.

"I didn't know myself. I only found out after your mother told me to call him over. I just thought he would be a typical DVD-*wallah*, you know, with no money, no family, no connections."

"He has money?" Honestly, it will be too unfair if he is rich also.

"To be frank, no. I haven't asked a lot. Doesn't look nice, *na*, to poke around too much. But from the things he's said, I think his mother works in a department store and the father is a salesman for a carpet company. They all moved to Toronto about six years ago. And they had to sell everything to make the move. Not like Jammy and Baby and all, who keep Canadian passport just in case. But don't tell anyone, please."

Department store. Salesman. Thanks God. I breathed out quietly. At least, he's not rich also. That would be just too much.

"So when's the wedding?" I asked, just to tease her.

"Irum's seventeen, for God's sake. She has to finish college first. And even though Zain is sweet and really, it was he who helped us look at everything differently and made us all so much happier, still we don't know his family or anything. To be honest, I'm not sure they're our sort of people. He's mentioned his aunt and cousins that he's staying with here and you know, I haven't heard of any one of them. Not even one. I don't think they move in our circles. And then Zain is also only eighteen. You know he wants to study films in college? Not business, not law but films. I mean, what a waste of time, no? What do you think it's like? You take exams on *Pretty Woman*? You do homework on the *Titanic*? No, I don't think Zain will ever be rich. Pity, you know, because he's so nice. No, I'm quite happy Irum meeting him in her own house under her parents' eyes but no talk of marriage please."

"Irum's okay with that?"

"You know that big hoo-ha she made about killing herself if we didn't allow her to marry him? Well, it was all drama. The minute I did what your Mummy said, and started inviting Zain and being nice to him, she never mentioned it again. I think he's also made it clear to her that this is just, you know, friendship."

"*Chalo*, Mulloo. It seems like it's all worked out for you, *haan*."

"But this catering business. I'm still not hundred per cent sure. I know lots of people are making so much in event managing, but don't you think people will say, 'Look at the poor thing, she has to work'?"

"If you really want the truth, Mulloo," I said carefully, "it's not something I would ever do."

"We all know that *you* don't have any talent. I was asking about *me*. But never mind, I'll ask Sunny instead. In any case, she knows more about the real world." And with that she picked up her big bottom from my bed and swinging her bag strap in her hand, bounced out before I could say anything. "Oh, by the way," she called from the door, "remember Tasbeeh, Farva's daughter? Last week she eloped with her cousin-brother, the one she'd had an engagement with. Thought you might like to know. Byeee."

Look at her! Saying I have no talent. And after everything I've done for her. Saving her from that fundo. Giving her Zain. Not taking her maid. And this is how she repays me. Mummy is right. Leopards never change their dots. I know what I'll do, I'll put it into Irum's head that she must marry Zain. That will serve Mulloo right. As soon as I recover from this dengue fever that's just what I'll do.

25 November

I think so, Jonkers has cracked. Properly and completely. He charged in all hot and panting into my sitting room, where worst luck, Janoo and Kulchoo were also sitting playing chess and burst out, "I'm marrying Sana. I proposed to her," he looked at his watch, "forty-two minutes ago."

"Wow!" said Janoo, looking up from the board. "Good on you."

"Congratulations, Uncle Jonkers." Kulchoo slapped him on the back.

"Don't be crack, Jonky," I said. "You can't."

"Who is Sana?" asked Janoo.

"She is the woman I love." Sometimes I think Jonky mistakes himself for Shahrukh in *Om Shanti Om*. The dialogues he gives!

"When's the wedding?" asked Kulchoo. "Can I be your *sarbala*? I quite fancy being your best boy. Also I'm running low on funds these days. Fifty thousand in presents from the extended family should do me nicely."

"Excellent. Jonkers, you have my vote of confidence," said Janoo, making a move on the board. "Good luck."

"Did you take permission from Aunty Pussy before?" I asked.

"No," said Jonkers.

"Well, then, you can't. Go back to Sana just now and tell her it was bad mistake because you forgot to ask your mother first."

"Why, in God's name, must he do that?" asked Janoo looking up from the board again.

"You play your game, *ji*," I snapped.

But Janoo, when he wants, can be as stubborn and as irritating as an ingrown hair.

"Explain yourself," Janoo said to me.

"You won't understand," I said.

"Try me."

"Yeah, Mum, explain yourself," said Kulchoo.

"My mother and even Apa here think that I'm incapable of finding a wife for myself. A suitable one that is," said Jonkers.

"And why is that?" Janoo looked at me.

I crossed my arms across my chest and looked away. "You know why," I muttered.

"Because Shumaila left me," Jonkers said.

"So?" said Kulchoo. "My friend Ahad's mum left his dad three times. And his mum isn't even—"

"It's not because Shumaila left," I said, ignoring Kulchoo. "In fact we *tau* give hundred, hundred thanks to God she ran away. It's because you *chose* her in the first place that worries us, Jonkers. Obviously you don't know what's what. So what did Sana say? I bet anything she must have jumped on you. Elderly girl like her—how old is she, twenty-nine? Thirty?— with no proposals. She *tau* must have thought it—"

"She said no."

"*What?*" I screeched. "Who does she think she is, *haan*? I bet you she is playing some game. To drive up her price."

"Mum!" yelled Kulchoo. "You can't speak about people like that."

"You mind your own business, *ji*," I snapped.

"No, really, it sucks!" said Kulchoo.

"Why did she refuse?" Janoo asked Jonkers.

"She said her mother and younger sister were financially dependent on her. And that she could not leave and set up home elsewhere and leave them to manage without her salary."

"See! See! Next thing she's going to ask is that Jonkers should take care of them all," I said. "Have it written down from me, next thing we'll see is Miss Sana and her whole family moving into Aunty Pussy's house and taking it over and shoving poor old Uncle and Aunty into the servants' quarters. And then don't say I didn't say."

"Could you please lower your voice?" Janoo said to me. "I can hear you perfectly well. So, Jonkers, what did you say to Sana then?"

Jonky said he told her that she could carry on with her job and in any case he had never intended to touch her earnings and that as far as he was concerned her money was her own and that she could dispose of it as she wanted. If she wanted to give every last *paisa* of it to her mother and sister that was her prer . . . perog . . . her business. But Sana had said that it didn't seem fair and that she couldn't accept. Jonkers had told her not to worry because he could afford it but still she said no, she couldn't become a burden on him and she wouldn't be able to spend his money with an easy conscious and so on and so fourth.

I still think it's all a drama to trap him good and proper. Just wait and see if I'm not right. Then Janoo asked what the up-short of it all was and Jonkers said that she had, after a lot of persuading from him, agreed to discuss it with her mother and that she would let him know what her mother said tomorrow.

"Mother will say, yes, yes, yes," I said. "I'm telling you from now only."

Janoo scowled at me but Jonkers turned really grateful eyes at me and said, "Really? You think so? I do hope you're right."

Crack.

"Jonky Uncle, may the force be with you," said Kulchoo.

But then it suddenly donned on me that if Sana's mother knows, she will loose no time in running around all of Lahore announcing her daughter's engagement to Jonkers, to make sure he can't go back on it after that. And Jonkers' hen will be cooked after that because obviously no decent-types with an illegible daughter would give second looks to Jonkers then. I tell you, these Sana-types are so slippery, so slippery that don't even ask. Like snakes in oil. Aunty Pussy must know immediately.

"Jonkers," I said, "Aunty Pussy must know immediately."

He shrugged. "Sure. I'm heading home now. I'll tell her. Not that her permission matters. I *am* going to marry Sana. Whether my mother likes it or not."

Something's happened to Jonkers. I think so it must be black magic. Someone's done it on him. He always used to be so obedient, so quiet. He didn't ask his mother before marrying Shumaila because I don't think so he had the guts. And between you, me, and the four walls, I think so it was Shumaila who marched him into the mosque. Knowing her, she didn't give him a choice. Jonkers just wasn't the type who'd have the nerves to go against his family like that. And now look at him. Being so pushy and all. It's definitely black magic, I'm telling you. Someone must have taken a hair or a nail cutting or something of his and done spells on it and knotted black threads or something. Or they must have slaughtered a black hen outside Aunty Pussy's house and done something with the blood. But who? To be honest, Sana doesn't look the type. And why would Shumaila bother now? Maybe it's just some spell that someone meant to put on someone else and it lost its way and came and got stuck to Jonkers instead. But no point telling Janoo about black magic because he will pooh-pooh it straight away. He's a septic *na*. Stuppid.

Janoo got up from his chair and put a hand on Jonkers' shoulder. "I wish you the very best and if there's anything I can do for you, let me know."

After Jonkers left I said to Janoo how he could encourage Jonkers like that? Did he have no sense of loyalty? He knew we didn't want this marriage. Who's we? he asked me. I said, me and Mummy and Aunty Pussy, who else? And he said that excuse me, but Jonkers' wishes mattered more. And in any case what had I against Sana? I hadn't even met her and I'd taken against her just like that. And I said, excuse *me ji*, but I *had* met her twice and once to talk to also. So he asked me what objection I had to her. And I said that who was I to object? If Jonkers wants, Jonkers can have. You know me, I said, last thing I do is spoil other people's fun. It's just that she's a nobody and probably a gold-dogger also. That's all.

"Jeez, Mum," said Kulchoo. "I'll pretend you didn't say that."

"You keep quiet," I shouted.

"You know what? You make me sick!" he shouted back.

And he stomped out of the room and slammed the door.

"See that?" I said to Janoo. "He talks to me like that because of *you*. You've turned him against me."

"He's reacting to what you are saying. Not what I'm saying," he said.

Then Janoo asked me to think back to when I'd met Sana. What about her behaviour had made me think that she was after Jonkers' money? So I thought back to that meeting in her office and her giving me coffee and agreeing to do my tickets so quickly and being so friendly and all and I said, she was too nice which proved she was after his money. Janoo wanted to know if she'd done flattery of me and I said no. He asked if she'd shown too much interest in me or my family, and who we were and whom we knew. I said no. And then he asked if she'd looked like she was sucking up to Jonkers. I remembered her ordering him back to his chair. So again, I said no.

"So why do you think she's up to no good then?"

So I told him then that the baggrounds didn't match.

For a long time he looked at the ceiling. He looked for so long that I also looked up. Were there some cracks in it? Holes? Spiders' webs? Then Janoo suddenly stopped looking. He held me by the elbows and said: That. Did. Not. Matter. What mattered was that the girl seemed nice and that Jonkers seemed to like her. And that was enough. They should be allowed to figure it out for themselves without other people jumping in with their wrong-headed suggestions. And what, I asked, if Jonkers was wrong like before? Then Jonkers would have to deal with it, he said. Had Jonkers asked me to deal with the fallout after Shumaila? No, I said, Jonkers didn't say one word even. But Aunty Pussy did. But did *Jonkers*? Janoo asked again. No, I said.

"Well then, let him be. It's important that he marries a partner. Someone with whom he feels at ease and whose company he enjoys and with whom he shares interests. Otherwise marriage can be a very lonely experience."

I looked at him. Then I asked, "Are you lonely?"

He didn't reply for a while. I could hear the gardener watering the plants outside our window. And then Janoo said, quietly, "Sometimes."

"I am also lonely," I whispered. "Not all the time. But sometimes."

"I know. I'm sorry."

He took a step towards me and touched my cheek. He tucked a lock of hair behind my ear. I covered his hand with my own and held it against my cheek. Just then, my stuppid mobile rang. Janoo shook his head at me but it was too late, I'd already picked it up. It was Mummy.

"Get over to Pussy's immediately." Her voice was so loud, I'm sure Janoo could also hear every word. "I'm on my way there also. She called me two seconds ago screaming and wailing, 'If you want to see me alive, come over at once.' Apparently Jonkers has found yet another blow-dryer and already proposed to her also and she's said yes and the marriage is tomorrow and Pussy says she'll kill herself before she attends."

Janoo stepped away from me. I didn't want him to go away. I wanted him to stay near me and talk to me and touch my face again and look at me like he had just before Mummy called. But suddenly I was shy. I also felt angry with Mummy for calling at that time.

"Oho, Mummy," I snapped, "the marriage is not tomorrow." But she had already put down the phone. "Listen," I said to Janoo. "I have to go now but when I come back we'll talk. Wait for me, please?"

I stopped only to put on some lipstick (Mac Russian Red) and spray on some scent (Channel No. 19) and put on some blush (Nars Terra Cota) and brush my hair (never know whose car you will pass on the way) and to tell Shameem to iron my grey sari with the blue flowers for tonight's dinner at Sunny's and also to put out my blue heels, not the Gina ones, the Prada ones, and then I was rushing out of the room. As I was rushing, Janoo called out behind me, "Remember what I told you! It's *his* life!"

26 November

Worst luck! Sana's mother wants Sana to marry *and* she wants to meet Jonkers' family. As Aunty Pussy said, "Why would she say no? It's not every day that a towelling empire and so much real state suddenly falls into your lap." Jonkers of course is being like the cow in that nursery rhyme. The one who jumped over the moon. Or did she jump over the spoon? Anyways, you know what I mean. That he is happy. Very, very happy.

He told me that Sana's mother wouldn't hear of her not marrying for her and her little sister's sake. She said that Sana had sacrificed enough already. Apparently when she came top in English Literature in her BA at Lahore College her father had really wanted Sana to go for her Masters to America. But after he died, she quietly dropped her studies and got this job and since then she's spent every penny she's earned on them and Sana's mother has always felt hugely guilty about that. So if now she'd found a man who liked her and she liked him, then her mother insisted she must marry him. Nothing would give her greater happiness. She and the little girl would be absolutely fine. Also, it seems, she's about to take over from the headmistress of her school who is retiring and so she's getting a raise and she feels she will be able to cope in that easily for her little daughter and herself and so Sana mustn't worry about them but think of herself. Jonkers is so happy, so happy that don't even ask.

Not like that night when I went over to his house after he'd told his mother and she was threating to slit her throat with the fruit knife and Jonkers quietly said, "Go ahead," and went to his room and shut the door. I wanted to run after Jonkers into his room because I think so he has an electric heater in there. But no, I had to sit with Mummy and Aunty Pussy in Aunty Pussy's freezing, dark lounge. There was this gas heater-type thing there which I think so she bought from a second-hand shop when Jonkers was born. It made guggling-type noises and gave off a gassy smell but no heat. I asked Aunty Pussy if we could bring in another heater, but she gave me an angry look and said, "The whole country's got no gas." I wanted to tell her that my house is also in the same country and we have gas, lots of gas, but Mummy gave me a warning look and so I didn't say anything but inside I thought to myself, "No wonder Shumaila ran away."

I think so when Jonkers told Aunty Pussy to go ahead and slit her throat if she wanted, he also knew that his mother being the miser that she is hadn't changed her knives for so long that they can't even slit the skin of a grape let alone her leathery old neck. Or maybe he really meant it. Maybe he's decided like Janoo said, that it's his life and his mother can do what she likes. He damn cares. That night Mummy and me, we sat there till one o'clock trying to talk with Aunty Pussy.

By the time I got home not only had I missed Sunny's dinner but Janoo was also asleep and I had such a spitting headache that I took two Lexxos and slipped into bed besides him. "Mmm, good to have you back," he murmured, and took me in his arms.

30 November

So much has been happening in my life lately with this Jonkers thing that I'd almost forgotten that big Eid was on top of our heads and that I hadn't done anything about sacrificing any sheep. Janoo wanted to give the sacrificing money to charity, to the IDPs or something, but I said no. We have to kill two sheep to keep evil eye off us. Of course I didn't say this to Janoo because he would have gone up in smoke but until Jonkers is married I'm not taking any risks with Kulchoo. I know Aunty Pussy is our relative and everything, but still. Thanks God, that's one thing Janoo's mother, the Old Bag, and I agree on: there's nothing like killing sheep to make God happy. And also, as good Muslims it is our duty to give sacrifice at Eid ul Azha. In fact, this time, what with my lucky escape and bombs everywhere and threats to Kulchoo's school and everything, I told the Old Bag to sacrifice three sheep. Not two. It's extra insurance.

The Old Bag took care of the sacrifices in Sharkpur, otherwise we would also have had to kill the sheep on our driveaway like fundo Farva and her powder-pasha husband and runaway daughter. But just look at Tasbeeh! That quiet little mouse turning out to be such a sharpie. But you know what? Good for her. In her place I'd have done same.

225

But big news is I've managed to convince Aunty Pussy there's no harm in meeting Sana's family. That way at least she could tell Jonkers honestly that she had done her bit and she'd gone along and seen the family and the girl and that she had *tau* even liked them as people, but that she didn't think they'd make a good match. And what to do, these things were in Allah's lap and what He didn't want, how could we force? And then Jonkers couldn't also say to her that she never gave it a chance. And maybe he'd give Sana up for his mother's sake. And maybe not. But of course, I didn't say it there. Mummy gave Aunty Pussy Mulloo's example who'd taken the wind out of Irum's sale by embracing her boyfriend with open arms. And she told Aunty Pussy that sometimes children do these things out of stubbornness and that best way is to always call their buff and go along pretending you are doing what they want but from inside doing the opposite.

Next morning when Janoo had asked me what had expired at Aunty Pussy's that night I'd told him that I'd convinced her to meet Sana's family. He patted me on the head and said, "Good girl." Like I was Lassie.

Jonkers says he's already met Sana's family. And they all love him and he them. Between you, me, and the four walls, I'm a bit double-minded about Sana. I don't have anything against her personally, but I feel maybe Jonkers could do a little bit better. Not much, but a little bit. And if you make me put my hand on the Holy Koran and swear on Kulchoo's life, then I will say that Sana is much nicer than both Tanya and Tasbeeh and with Miss Shumaila *tau* there is no comparison and obviously Irum doesn't count, but it's just the bagground, if you know what I mean. When all the girls in my kitty will ask, "So who did your cousin marry then?" and I say Sana Raheem, I know what they'll say. "From which family?" And I'll have to say "From no family." And they'll think, "Poor things, couldn't even get a decent family." Anyways, tomorrow we are to go and have tea with them. The Raheems, not my kitty group. I swear I'm getting quite fed up with having tea with Jonkers' in-laws. Bore.

1 December

The house was small. Even smaller than I was fearing it would be. On Aunty Pussy's insistence, we went in Janoo's Prado jeep to show them what's what. I swear the road—no, alley—on which Sana's house is, is so narrow, so narrow that a cyclist who was coming the other way from us had to get off his cycle and press himself into a hedge to make room for us and our Prado to pass. I don't know why Sana and all bother to have a gate because it's so small, even I could jump over it. In my D&G platforms. Janoo's driver got out and rang the bell and when no guard came, gave the gate a good shake and it looked as if would fall off its winges. So thin and weak it was.

"Are you noting?" said Aunty Pussy, wrinkling her nose as if she'd smelt a bad smell.

Then a maid—not a guard, but a maid—came out drying her hands on her *dupatta* and she opened the gate and the drive was so narrow and so short that our car took up the whole of it and the maid could hardly close the gate behind us. In front of us was parked one white Suzuki like we have at home for our servants to go and do shopping in the bazaar. The front garden—I don't think so there's a back one—was the size of my bathroom at home. But if I was to put my hand on the Holy Koran I'd have to say that it wasn't too bad. A big shady-type tree, jasmine bushes, a wooden bench and half tap, half fountain-type thing set into a wall that flowed into a stone basin. Sound of water was all tinkly, tinkly, soft, soft.

"Let's get this over with quickly," muttered Aunty Pussy, leading the way.

I wanted to tell her to please be nice-ish but just then the same maid opened the door. God knows where their other servants were hiding. A tall, middle-aged-type woman with short, grey hair stood in the hall. I say hall, but it was actually the size of my wardrope back home. She was wearing a plain biscuit-coloured *shalwar kameez* and a woollen shawl with brown stripes on it. Not *shahtoosh*. Or even pashmina. Just plain wool. She greeted us nicely and told us she was Zahra, Sana's mother. She led us into her sitting room.

Windows were big. Walls were white. Sofas and chairs were also covered in white cotton. Bright cotton *dhurries* were scattered on the floor. There were four or five big paintings on the walls—all of skies. Dawn skies. Dust skies. Morning skies. Night skies. And lots and lots of lilies in vases all round the room. I think so they must have been given by Jonkers because he'd given the same buffet of foreign lilies to me when I'd had my counter with the beardo. Aunty Pussy scowled when she saw them because I think so she also guessed. Must be doing mental sums of how much they must have cost. Room didn't have too many decoration pieces. A few things of old brass, not silver, but nicely polished. One thing I will say, but. Room was very, very clean. The floor beamed, the table tops shone, walls were spotless. Poor things, must have scrubbed and scrubbed, getting ready for us. Couldn't be getting too many important guests.

We sat down and then Sana and her little sister came in. Little sister wore braces and glasses and a blue frock. Not a beauty from anywhere. Aunty Pussy's eyes narrowed when she saw Sana. So did Mummy's. Sana was dressed all in white. Like a nurse. All she needed was a white cap on her head and a clock pinned to her chest. But thanks God, hair was loose. She looked better that way, nose didn't look so long and face not so bony. She smiled and greeted Aunty Pussy and Mummy and they replied with small unsmiling nods. Sana came up to me and I got up and kissed her on the cheek. Behind her back, Aunty Pussy gave me a cold stare. I hope so Sana's mother didn't see.

Zahra said how nice it was that the winter had finally come. Didn't they think that the summer had been unusually long this year?

"No," said Aunty Pussy.

Zahra laughed and said it must be her imagination then.

"Yes," said Aunty Pussy.

I asked the sister who was sitting beside me, what her name was.

"Noor," she said. "I'm eleven. I'm in Class 6 at New Dawn School. Do you have any children?"

"Yes. One. He's fifteen."

"What's his favourite subject at school?"

"I think so he likes doing computers best."

"Mine's art. Like my Ammi's. She's an artist, you know. She painted all these." Noor nodded at the pictures on the walls.

Zahra shook her head. "Thank you, darling, but I'm no artist. I just put these up to cover the walls. Actually I'm an art teacher," she said to us.

"Where do you teach?" asked Mummy.

"New Dawn School. The Gulberg branch."

"I know the owner," said Aunty Pussy. "Zeenat Kuraishi. One of my closest friends."

Haw, look at Aunty Pussy. What a show-offer. And liar also, I'm sorry to say.

"Mrs. Kuraishi's been very kind to me," said Zahra. "When Noor was little she suffered from bad asthma and I had to take time off school whenever she was ill, which was often. But not once did Mrs. Kuraishi dock my salary or put any pressure on me. She knew my circumstances and was endlessly understanding."

"You can always tell people from a good family," sniffed Aunty Pussy.

"And now Mrs. K. is making Ammi headmistress," said Noor. "She will have her own office with air conditioner. And a secretary also."

"Shush," laughed Sana.

The maid came in with drinks. It was freshly squeezed pomegranate juice. Aunty Pussy sighed as she took hers, as if she was being offered medicine. I took a small sip of mine. It was cold and sweet in a sharpish way. Better than I expected.

At least they know how to make juice, I thought. When the maid left I asked Sana how her friend—Shabnam's daughter—was doing since her die-vorce. Sana said that she was quite shaken up and a bit depress also, but that was only to be expected. To have such a talk-of-the-town wedding and then such a public die-vorce must be very difficult.

"If people are going to rush into unsuitable marriages without looking left or right," said Aunty Pussy heavily, "they should prepare themselves for disasters."

There was a short silence after that and then Sana's mother said how lovely it had been to meet Jonkers and what a sensitive and generous man he was and how proud Aunty Pussy must be of him.

"He brought Sana all these flowers," said Noor. "And a big slab of Toblerone for me. Biggest I've ever seen."

Aunty Pussy looked as if she'd been stabbed. "Unfortunately, he's always wasted money. Doesn't know with what difficulty it is made."

Sana turned red—or as red anyone can get if they are darkish—but she didn't say anything.

Mummy quickly asked Zahra how long she had worked at Zeenat's school.

"Seven years. Ever since my husband passed away."

"Jonkers told me your husband died in a car accident," I said.

"Yes," replied Zahra. "He was driving back from Multan. It was late at night. He crashed into a tree. After all these years, I still can't understand how it happened. He was such a careful driver. Either he must have swerved to avoid some unexpected object on the road or he must have fallen asleep at the wheel." Her voice wobbled a bit.

Noor got up from besides me and went and sat next to her mother. She put her hand on her mother's knee. Zahra covered it with her own.

"Noor must have been very small then," I said.

"She was four," said Zahra.

"Big age difference between your daughters," said Mummy.

Zahra nodded. "My husband wanted a big family but after Sana was born I wasn't able to conceive again. We were disappointed but accepted, eventually, that it was not to be. In any case, Sana was everything we could have wished for," she smiled at Sana, "and more. But then suddenly after eighteen years, along came Noor. We were thrilled. My husband used to call her his bonus."

"You must have been quite old then," said Aunty Pussy.

Honestly! If I'd been Zahra, I'd have said not as old as you are, *ji*. But she just laughed.

"Yes, I was forty-three. I couldn't believe it myself."

"You must have been very embarrassed, your mother giving birth when you were so old?" Aunty Pussy said to Sana.

"Not at all," Sana replied, coldly. "It was what I wanted more than anything else. To have a brother or a sister."

I got up. "Excuse me, can I go to the toilet?"

"I'll take you." Noor jumped up.

She led me down a tight little corridor to a twin bedroom. "This is Ammi's and my room. Sana Apa, she has her own. All to herself. Bathroom's there." She pointed to a door leading off it. "Shall I wait for you?"

"Thanks, but no need. I'll be back in a minute."

So no guest powder room even.

After Noor had gone I had a good look around the bedroom. It was same as sitting room. Very clean and tidy but nothing expensive anywhere. No flat-screen TV, no silk curtains, no wooden floor, no Persian rug, no velvet sofa. Old window-type AC instead of new split-types we all have in our homes. The beds were covered with cotton blue-and-white bedspreads that matched the curtains. Both were faded and old-looking. On one bed—I think so must be Noor's—was a raggedy teddy bear.

One whole wall was covered with shelves filled from top to toe with books. Not hardback expensive books like Janoo's but tattery paperbacks, like you can buy from the second-hand stalls on the footpaths of Anarkali bazaar. The other wall had framed photos all over it. I went up to the photos wall. On top were the oldish ones, with faded colours and people in past-it fashions.

Zahra dressed as a bride, smiling shyly at her groom. He, with longish nose and darkish face, turbaned and in a *sher-wani*, his head thrown back and laughing. A young-looking Zahra, with long, loose hair looking down at a baby (must be Sana only) in her arms. A teenaged Sana, skinny and in glasses, receiving some prize at school. Sana, still skinny and still in glasses, dressed in white PE uniform with a racket in one hand and a silver cup in the other, posing stiffly. The father—in pant-shirt—standing besides her, a hand on her shoulder. Father now with greyish hair, carrying a baby girl on his shoulders. The girl guggling and pulling the father's hair in her fat fists. The whole family on a picnic—Noor, a toddler now, in her mother's lap, Sana sitting next to her father, her legs drawn up, scowling at the camera. A child's birthday party—must be Noor's only—with Sana and her father in paper hats eating off the same plate.

And then, near the bottom of the wall, there's no more father. A little Noor, wearing a too-big school frock, with a satchel across her chest, clutching Sana's hand. Probably Noor's first day at school. I have a photo like that of Kulchoo at home. Janoo holds his one hand and I hold the other. A slightly older Noor in white PE uniform holding a silver cup with Sana smiling proudly by her side. Noor, Sana, and Zahra on a beach with palm trees in the bagground. This must be the holiday Sana told me about at her office, because all are looking same like they do now. Noor and Sana, in swimsuits and wet hair, giggling, but Zahra looking away, out to the sea.

I sat down on a bed. It was the one with the teddy. One of the teddy's eyes was missing and one ear was all patchy-patchy as if the fur had been rubbed off. As I sat there with the teddy in my lap, something happened to me. You know how when you see a picture in a magazine and you think it's just a tree but when you hold the picture away and look at it again you realize that there's the face of a woman hidden inside it? The lower branches are her chin and jaw and the upper branches are her forehead and that row of leaves are her eyebrows and this line of leaves are her lips and the shaggy leaves at the top are her hair and the tree trunk is her neck. And once you see the picture like that, I mean you see the face hidden inside, you can't see the tree any more, even if you try? It was bit like that for me with Sana and her family. In the bedroom I began to see them differently. Not as Aunty Pussy wanted me to see them but as Jonkers saw them.

And I realized what Janoo told me when my accident-type thing happened with the *jihadi* is right—things come and go. But people, once they go, they don't come back. They just leave a hole. The father had left a hole in the lives of the people in this house. But Sana was doing her best to fill that hole for her mother and sister. And without doing any look-at-me-what-a-heroine-I-am drama. Jonkers was right—she was brave and feasty and loving. She was the kind of girl you wanted on your side when you got into a fight at school. Because she would stand by you, and no matter how many girls you were up against, she would fight for you and if you lost the fight, then she would comfort you and tell you that it didn't matter and make you laugh and forget your fight. Jonkers had chosen well. Sana would make him a good partner. She would make him feel that, whatever happened, she would be there for him. Like Janoo is for me.

When I came back to the sitting room, tea was being given. Noor, looking like she was going to burst into tears any minute, was passing plates around and a stone-faced Zahra was pouring out the tea. Sana was sitting on the edge of her seat, her back ram-road straight, her hands gripping the chair's seat. Mummy was looking down at her hands. Aunty Pussy, in her cheetah print polyester suit and her back-combed maroon hair, was the only one who looked pleased with herself. She was relaxing in her armchair, hundred per cent easy. At once I knew Aunty Pussy had said something bad. I told you, *na*, that I have a sick-sense. Also I know what Aunty Pussy's like.

"Ooh, is that tea?" I said. "Can I have a cup?"

"Of course," said Zahra. "Do you take sugar?"

"One, please. Thank you, Noor. These sandwiches, they look so yummy. I bet you made them!"

"No," she giggled. "Ammi did. But I helped her with mixing the cake mix."

"Then I must try some of that also."

Aunty Pussy looked at me and frowned slightly. I ignored.

"Mmm, so light! Better even than Masoom Bakery's."

Aunty Pussy's head snivelled around at me. She gave me a glare. Let her. I damn cared.

"Jonkers—we call Jehangir Jonkers at home, *na*—he hasn't stopped talking about your hospitality, Zahra Apa," I said. "Now I know why."

There was a strange choking-type sound from Aunty Pussy's side but I didn't bother looking. Mummy also gave a small cough but her also I ignored.

"Has Sana told you, Zahra Apa, that I went to meet her at her office with Jonkers? *Haw*, Aunty Pussy, did I forget to mention to you? Imagine! How absent-minded I've become. What a fab office. And her desk. Bigger and higher than anybody else. And so many people working under her also. You must be *so* proud of her, Zahra Apa."

"I am. *Very* proud of her," said Zahra, looking straight at Aunty Pussy.

Aunty Pussy put her cup down with a thud. "We have to be going now—"

"I'm having my tea still, Aunty." I made no move to get up. Nor was I going to.

"Finish quickly. I have to be getting home."

"Why?" I asked. "What's the rush?"

"Kaukab is at home," she snapped. As if he ever goes out anywhere.

"He'll be fine, Pussy," said Mummy. Aunty Pussy gave her a killer look. Good. Mummy was moving to my side also. About time.

And then Mummy said to Sana, "What do you do, *beta*?"

"I run a travel agency."

"Must be lot of responsibility and hard work also," said Mummy.

"She works ver-*ry* hard," said Noor. "Goes in the morning and doesn't come home till the evenings. Sometimes she gets so late that Mummy and I, we get so worried, we wait at the gate. Mummy says we mustn't call, because she is probably busy. But on Sundays we have fun, don't we, Apa? We go swimming and we play tennis and carom and watch movies and—"

"Swimming? Tennis? *Here*?" Aunty Pussy looked unbelievably around the small room as if Noor had said they shoot Bollywood films there every Sunday.

"Obviously not in this room, Pussy," said Mummy.

"My late husband was a member of Punjab Club," said Zahra. "After he passed away I applied for membership. It was our one luxury but I was determined not to give it up. It was what my husband would have wanted. He was very sporty himself and encouraged the girls to do lots of sport."

"We also did snorkelling in Langkawi last year and Apa even went diving," added Noor. "They didn't let me dive because I was too little. But Apa promised me when I was sixteen, she'd take me again. Didn't you?"

"My Jonkers had asthma as a child," announced Aunty Pussy. "So I never let him play any games. And he's not one bit interested in it either. I also think it's waste of time. And money."

"My husband and son *tau* just love it," I said quickly. "They also play tennis and go swimming and when they go to the village they do riding—on horses you know—"

"You have *horses*?" squealed Noor.

"Yes, in my husband's village. I don't go there much because I find it a bit bore to be honest, but if you like I'll take you all. You must come and stay, Zahra Apa, you and Sana and Noor. I think so, you'll like it. There are lots of skies there that you can paint. And, Sana, you like wildlife, don't you? There's loads of cows and sheep and horses and goats there. You must come, definitely. Maybe in Christmas holidays? Or even better, on the weekend because, honestly, I can't take more than three days of village. I'm not like you, Sana, into nature and things. Sorry *haan*? You must meet my husband, by the way. I don't know why, but I have a feeling that both of you will get along very well."

Sana laughed and Zahra said thank you, I was very kind and Noor asked if we could go next weekend and Mummy smiled and Aunty Pussy suddenly stood up and said angrily, "I'm leaving. Goodbye." And walked out.

Let her go, I thought. Let her sit in the car and steam in her own anger. Good radiance! But then Mummy also slowly got to her feet with a sorry-type smile and said that she had enjoyed meeting them all very much and that the tea had been very nice and that she better go after Pussy because she hasn't been feeling very well, *na*. So then I stood up also but I didn't give a sorry-type smile and I didn't make any loser-type excuses. Not at all. I kissed Sana and I kissed Noor and I went up to Zahra Apa and I took her hands in mine and I looked her in the eyes and told her what a lovely family she had and how lucky Jonkers would be to become a part of it. If they wanted him, that was. Because you know something? Suddenly I knew where I stood. And it certainly wasn't with Aunty Pussy. It was with Jonkers and Janoo.

"Drop me at home," Aunty Pussy ordered in the car.

"No, you're coming home with me," I said. "And Mummy, you too." I must have said it in a dictator-type voice because neither of them did any arguing.

Once I got home, I took them to the sitting room, called Ameena, sorry Shameem, and told her to tell anyone who called for me that I wasn't home and then I told the bearer to tell the guards the same outside and I sat Mummy and

Aunty Pussy down and then I gave them some pieces of my mind.

I told them I knew how upset they'd been at Jonkers' secret marriage to Miss Shumaila. I had been also. I also knew how much they wanted him to marry a nice rich girl from a nice rich bagground. I had wanted it also. But if I was to put my hand on Kulchoo's head and say truthfully why I'd wanted it, it was because I thought it would make my name heavy in the world and get me more respect from my kitty group. I wasn't thinking of Jonkers' happiness, I was thinking of my own. And okay there might be some very nice rich girls hiding in the world somewhere but the two or three we had met were not right for Jonkers. And the girl that he had found for himself was just right—strong, brave, loyal, and loving. She would be on his side.

"Yes," snapped Aunty Pussy. "Like that thief Shumaila was on his side."

"Pussy," said Mummy. "Shumaila is over. I'm sure Jonkers also knows now that she was not right for him."

"You can stop lecturing me, you mother and daughter. What about all the other two-bit girls that he liked before and would have married, *married*, if I hadn't saved him?"

"Maybe, Aunty Pussy, he's never felt comfortable with the types you wanted for him," I said. "Because he had nothing to say to them and he wasn't their type either. Tell me, what could he have said to that rude, spoilt Tanya? *Haan?* She didn't even bother to look at him, let alone make talk with him. Had he married her he would always have been like a servant in their house. And as for that poor Tasbeeh, she looked so unhappy herself, you honestly think she was going to make *him* happy? And you remember that day he came to the wedding with us to look at the girls we thought were right for him, he looked so uncomfortable, standing behind your seat, suffering silently in his suit."

"He was comfortable with Shumaila? With her stealing his car? And my jewels?"

"Again, Pussy," sighed Mummy. "Again you're bringing up Shumaila. She's in the past. Look at the future."

"At what? At a two-bit travel agent?"

"Yes," I said, "at a travel agent. Who Jonkers is proud of. Who he loves and respects."

"How can he respect someone with no standing, no name?"

"Sometimes, Pussy," said Mummy in a tired voice, "sometimes we have to forget all those things and think only of our child's happiness."

"Fine coming from you," shouted Aunty Pussy, "you with your Oxford-educated, wealthy son-in-law from an old landed family. I'm sorry but I'm not allowing Jonkers to marry Sana in my house. If he wants another miserable wedding in a mosque he's welcome to it."

"He won't have to, Aunty Pussy," I said. "Because he can get married from *my* house. Mine and Janoo's. We'll be proud to host his wedding to Sana."

"You! You! You traitor!" shouted Aunty Pussy. She picked up her bag and rushed out of the room.

"Oh, *beta*," sighed Mummy. "Think before you speak like

that. You remember what happened to Kulchoo last time you got into a thing with Pussy? You have just one child. Go after her and say sorry."

"I damn care," I said.

But between you, me, and the four walls, I'd totally forgotten about Kulchoo's accident that had started this thing in the first place. "That was an accident," I said, crossing my fingers behind my back and quickly saying a prayer for Kulchoo's safety under my breaths. "And besides, I'm not supercilious any more."

That night as Kulchoo slept in his bed, I crept into his room on tiptoe and stood by his pillow and said three special prayers from the Holy Koran, to keep away black magic and evil eyes, then I blew on Kulchoo from his head to his foot three times making sure the prayers covered his whole body. There! Now we were safe!

18 December

Last Tuesday was Jonkers' wedding. In our front lawn. It was tiny. Just two hundred people. But even if I say it with my own mouth, it was very tastily done. Mulloo arranged it. It was a favour I did her, giving her her first do as an event manager. But by now you must be knowing that I'm like that— soft headed, charitable soul. By the way, I also beat Sunny to it, and now everyone in my kitty group will remember how it was me and not Sunny who launched Mulloo's carrier as an event manager. And must say, Mulloo did it very nicely even though she organized whole thing in one week. Because once Sana agreed and Zahra agreed, then Jonkers wanted to get married straight away and as Janoo said: "Why ever not?"

So it was mad rush because we had to fit it in before Muharram but I think so, we managed. One good thing about marrying someone who is not so well-reknowned is that your guest list is small and also Jonkers and Sana are not the big splashy dowry-type people, so we didn't have to wait for months having furniture made to order and special sets of jewellery brought from India and bags and shoes from London and Dubai and so on and so fourth.

The flowers were all local—pink roses and mauve glads—and

the garden was lit with pink fairy lights. Don't ask me how but Mulloo found a mauve velvet tent-type thing from somewhere and we put that up in the front lawn and spattered small, small tables all around with rose petals and white table-cloths and pink candles. And it was all warm and smug inside because we had those standing-up heater-type things—I think so they're called brassieres.

Zain did the music and Kulchoo and Farhad and Irum brought all their friends and there was non-stop dancing for three full nights. Even Sunny and Akbar and Baby and Jammy and Nina and Maha joined in, and Jonkers and Janoo played hosts. There was only one dish because bore guvmunt order is still in place, in fact it's become worst, but no one complained because it was Mulloo's famous mutton *karahi* and anyways, everyone had had so much of wine that they were past caring.

Even Zeenat came and she was very nice about it and gave Jonkers and Sana a beautiful painting. I wore a fab new outfit in pink and mauve, designer of course, with grey contacts (green is so past it) and a ruby necklace and matching earrings. I'd have ordered a Tarun Tahliani sari for myself from India with Sarvoski crystals but there was a time problem, *na. Chalo*, at Kulchoo's wedding then. I also wanted Sana to buy a fab new outfit from a designer, ready-made unfortunately, because again we didn't have time to order. It was to be Janoo's and my present, *na*, but she said no, she wanted to wear her mother's wedding clothes. She wore a cream and gold *gharara* and between you, me, and the four walls, it was a bit old-fashioned and a bit on the simple side but she carried it away.

And Zahra wept and Noor danced and Jonkers grinned so much that I thought his face would break in two. By the way, he was wearing such a nice Italian wool suit, that don't even ask. Charcole gray, with a deep, rich sheen. And without his glasses and his old nervous way of gulping-shulping, he actually looked quite dishy. Promise, by God, I'm not joking.

Mummy tried very hard to make Aunty Pussy come but you know, *na*, that she is proud, stubborn-type and said till the last minute that she would come over her own dead body. I said to Jonkers, *chalo*, never mind she'll come around when you have your first child. But on the day of the *nikah* she suddenly turned up with poor old Uncle Kaukab in toe. She brought her old diamond necklace—a bit dirty looking because as usual she'd saved on the polishing—and she put it around Sana's neck and she didn't say anything but she took Sana's face in her hands and kissed Sana's forehead. And Uncle Kaukab put a shaking hand on Jonkers' head and said, "All my love and blessings, always."

Between you, me, and the four walls, I was a little bit edgy about the security. More bombs burst last week. One in DG Khan that killed twenty-four. Another in Peshawar that I don't know killed how many. And more shootings in Karachi. In a mosque. Janoo was looking at the papers the day before the wedding and he said in his special Doomday voice, "This year more people have died in bombs and shootings in Pakistan than in Iraq. What will become of us?"

"Now don't do talk like that," I said. "We have to be happy. We have a wedding in our house. We can't go around looking depress. Doesn't look nice."

But thanks God everything went off okay at our wedding. And when Janoo and I were standing together and watching Sunny and Kulchoo doing the twist and a drunken Tony waving his glass and pottering around them and wolf-whistling, and an embarrassed Irum hiding behind her laughing mother, Janoo put his arm around me and said, "Still want to move to Dubai?"

I looked up at him and said, "Maybe not tonight."

And then I asked, "Still feeling lonely?"

He laughed and dropping a kiss on top of my head, he said, "Maybe not tonight."

Yesterday we had our kitty (it was Mulloo's turn to host this time) and all the girls said that even if the wedding was small it was lovely, like olden times when it used to be just nears and dears and not thousands of distants. I looked carefully at their faces just to see if they were being fakely nice, but I think so, they meant it. And Mulloo's got lots more bookings because of me and so I told her: "Mulloo *yaar*, don't forget, *haan*, how I started your business?"

Jonkers has taken Sana on a safari to a place called Boats Wana for their honeymoon. In her place I'd have chosen London or Singapore for the shopping but no, she said, she wanted to commute with nature. Crack! Janoo gave her a fab-type camera and she flew over the moon with happiness. Double crack! And Janoo and Kulchoo both said to Jonkers and Sana that come and show us the pictures when you return and then maybe we'll all go next year as well. I'll go over my dead body to a jungle to watch dirty, smelly animals, I said under my breaths but on top I smiled and said, "*Haan*, what a fab idea!" And then

I thought to myself, "Why not?" So I said to Jonkers and Sana, "Make sure to find a nice five-stars-*wallah* hotel because I'm not staying in some horrid camp-shamp."

While Jonkers and Sana are away, Mummy and I are getting Aunty Pussy to paint the house and change the sofas which sag when you sit on them and also to shampoo the Persian carpets whose designs you can't see any more and hang new curtains and buy new heaters and make it all nice and ready for the bride's home-coming. Also, I've forced her to get poor old Ghulam a new set of fake teeth. Of course, Aunty Pussy grumbled a bit at first about the expense on the house but I think so secretly she's quite happy. One, because everybody praised the bride and said how pretty and natural she looked and two, it turns out everyone who matters to Aunty Pussy knows and likes Sana because they've all been buying their tickets from her for ever and also because Sana wants to keep working at her job and although on top she said "What's the need?," inside Aunty Pussy's very happy that she will be earning her keeps. And lastly, Zeenat Kuraishi told Aunty Pussy that she was lucky to have people as special as Sana and Zahra as part of her family and you know, *na*, that whatever Zeenat says is holy Braille for Aunty Pussy. So, between you, me, and the four walls, Aunty Pussy and Sana might have a few fights at first—because Aunty Pussy is bossy and Sana is not taking-it-quietly type—but you wait and see, after a while, they'll get along fine. Oh yes, and Jonkers and Sana will be very happy. How do I know? *Haw*, haven't I told you? I have a sick-sense about these things. Didn't I tell you Jonkers would find a girl at the Butt–Khan wedding? Past your mind back . . .

Acknowledgments

My thanks to Tash Aw, Carla Power, and Homa Rastegar Driver for their time, attention, and encouragement. And my gratitude to my agent, David Godwin, for his unflagging enthusiasm and to my editor of Broadway Paperbacks, Kate Kennedy, for her wisdom and humor. My thanks, also, to all the patient folk at Observatory Capital, in whose office *Duty Free* was written.

Reading Group Guide

1. *Duty Free* is set in Lahore, Pakistan, a bustling urban center. At first glance, the sphere that our protagonist lives and moves in looks much like it would in any large global city, from New York to London to Dubai. How does this presentation of Lahore match your expectations? How does it differ from the city you envisioned?

2. Our heroine is wonderfully absorbed in the details of her own life, to the point that she seems to willfully ignore the social, political, and economic upheaval just outside her front door. Each chapter begins with headlines from the local newspaper, and the juxtaposition between the very real, very dire situation in Pakistan and the often quite superficial preoccupations of our narrator provide ripe fodder for social satire. How does this compare to other fiction you have read? Do you feel the narrator is more or less sympathetic by the end of the novel?

3. In several places in the book, our protagonist discusses the importance of maintaining a home outside of Pakistan and of having foreign passports, should the family need to leave Pakistan

quickly. After our narrator and Mulloo are mugged, she asks Janoo if they can leave Pakistan and go somewhere "safe." Janoo tells her that "if we were to move, you would always miss this place. It is our home and without it we'd be homeless." Which position is the selfish one? Which position is the right one? Can "home" be created anywhere, or is it tied to the earth and the sky?

4. How is America's relationship with Pakistan perceived by the characters in *Duty Free*?

5. Our narrator met and married her husband through a traditional, arranged marriage, while her cousin Jonkers was determined to find his own mate. At first, our protagonist seems unsympathetic to those who buck the system, but by the end of the novel, she has helped both Irum and Zain and Jonkers and Sana be together. Why does she help these couples? How does her view of love and marriage change over the course of the novel? How has this changed her relationship with her own husband?

5. Do you think that our protagonist and her husband, Janoo, are a good match? Do they have a happy marriage?

6. How do family structures, as seen in *Duty Free*, differ from those in America? Do you think Pakistani family members are more supportive of each other or more controlling? Would you like to belong to such a family?

7. Moni Mohsin has been called a modern-day Jane Austen. How do the themes and characters in *Duty Free* mirror those in Austen's best-known works?

8. At the beginning of the novel, it appears as if the women in modern Lahore are defined by their relationships to others: by being good daughters, wives, mothers, friends. As the novel progresses, we see more and more examples of women demonstrating their own agency and economic freedom by becoming independent business owners and breadwinners for their families. Did any of these women surprise you? What are the ramifications of Sana's success? Mulloo's? Jameela's?

9. What is the family's relationship to the "bore" village? What is their responsibility to the people who live there?

10. Our narrator speaks in a language all her own, rife with malapropisms and misspellings. The effect is often quite funny, but there are moments when her descriptions are even more telling and accurate. What are some of your favorite examples?

About the Author

Moni Mohsin is the author of the Indian bestseller *The Diary of a Social Butterfly* and the award-winning *The End of Innocence*. Her writing has appeared in *The Friday Times, The Times, Guardian, Washington Post, Prospect, The Nation*, and many other publications. Born in Pakistan, she currently lives in London. *Duty Free* is her American debut.